AN ORIGINAL GRAPHIC NOVEL

THE DRAGON PRINCE

Through the Moon

Story by **AARON EHASZ**
and **JUSTIN RICHMOND**

Written by **PETER WARTMAN**

Illustrated by **XANTHE BOUMA**

An Imprint of **SCHOLASTIC**

wonderstorm

All rights reserved. Published by Scholastic Inc., *Publishers since 1920.* SCHOLASTIC and
associated logos are trademarks and/or registered trademarks of Scholastic Inc.

The publisher does not have any control over and does not assume any responsibility
for author or third-party websites or their content.

This book is a work of fiction. Names, characters, places, and incidents are either the
product of the author's imagination or are used fictitiously, and any resemblance to
actual persons, living or dead, business establishments, events, or locales is entirely
coincidental.

ISBN 978-1-338-60881-6 (paperback)

10 9 8 7 6 5 4 3   22 23 24

Printed in the U.S.A.   40

Edited by Chloe Fraboni, Rachel Stark, and Katie Woehr

Book design by Betsy Peterschmidt

Letters by Olga Andreyeva

Additional assistance with colors by Cynthia Cheng, Farrah Su, Boya Sun,
Adeetje Bouma, Eva Cone, Katie Mitroff

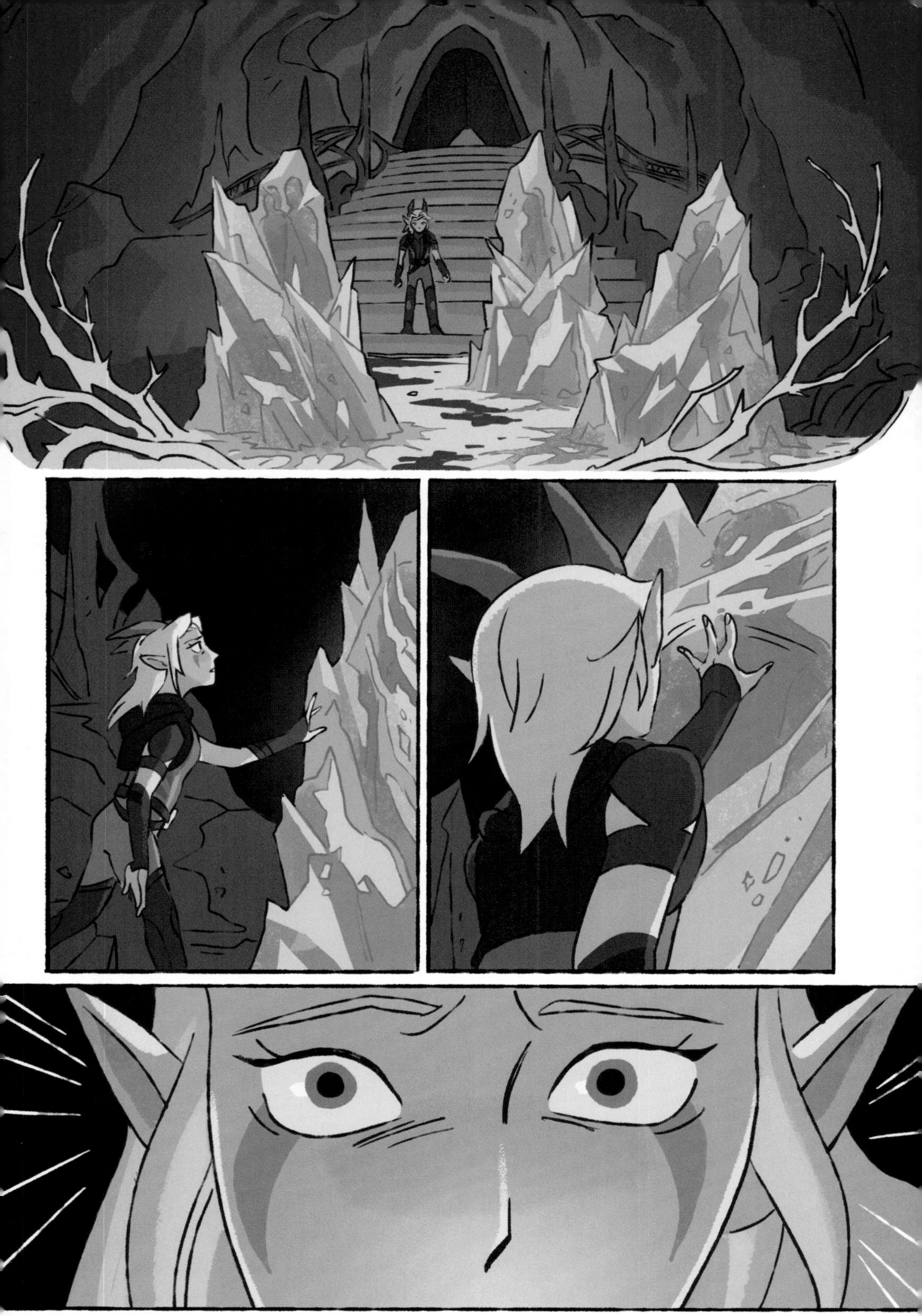

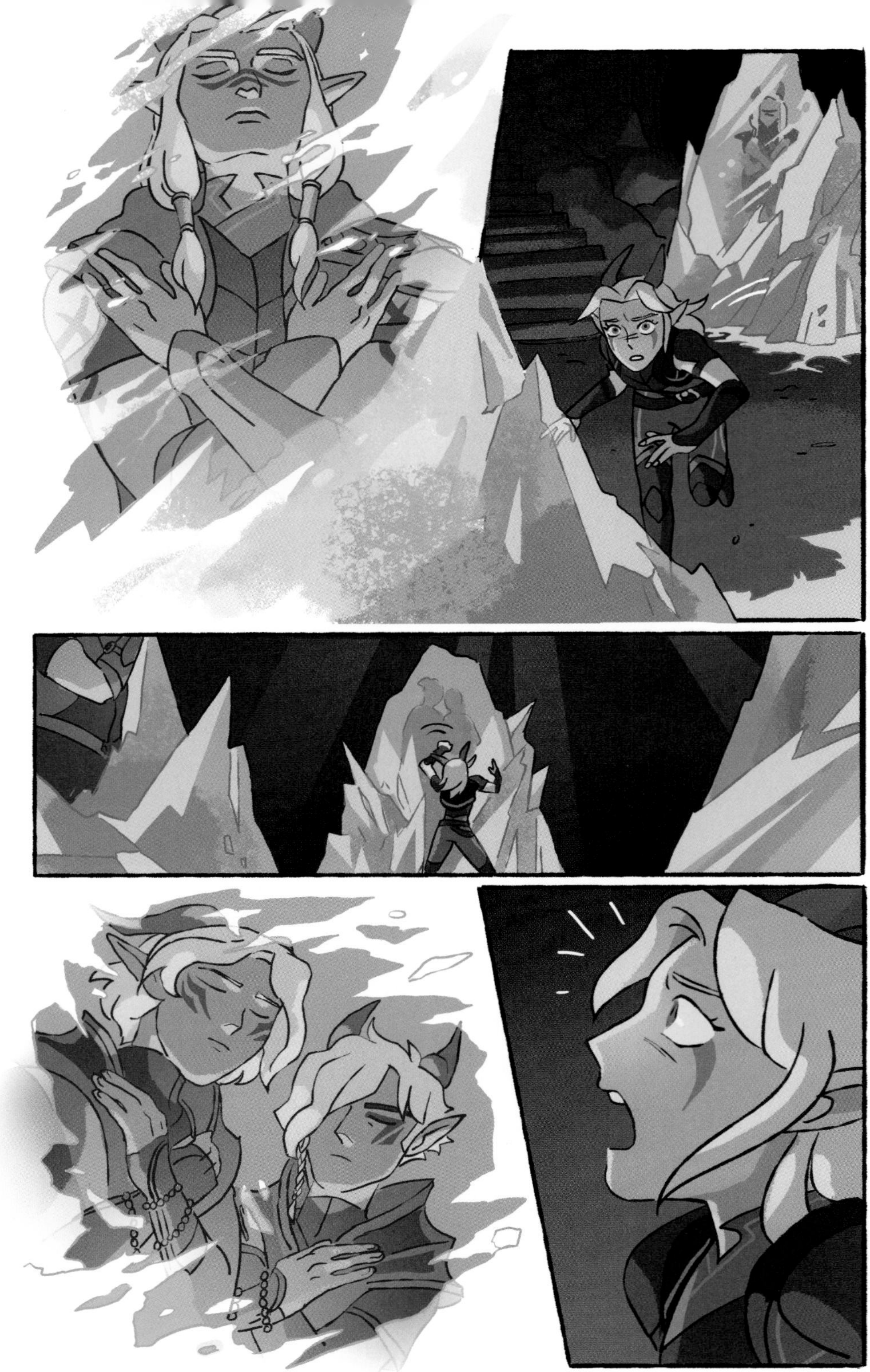

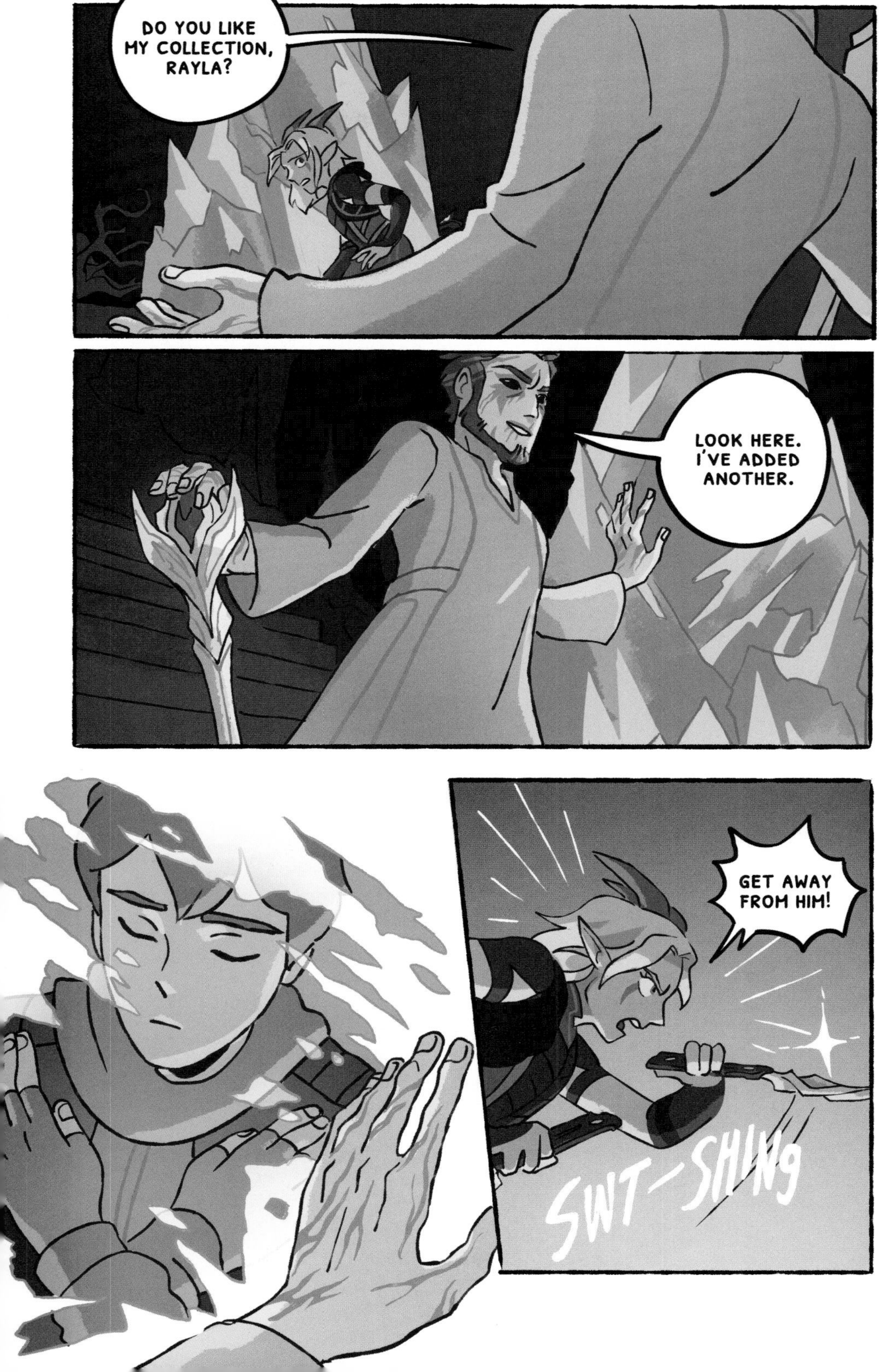
DO YOU LIKE MY COLLECTION, RAYLA?
LOOK HERE. I'VE ADDED ANOTHER.
GET AWAY FROM HIM!
SWT-SHING

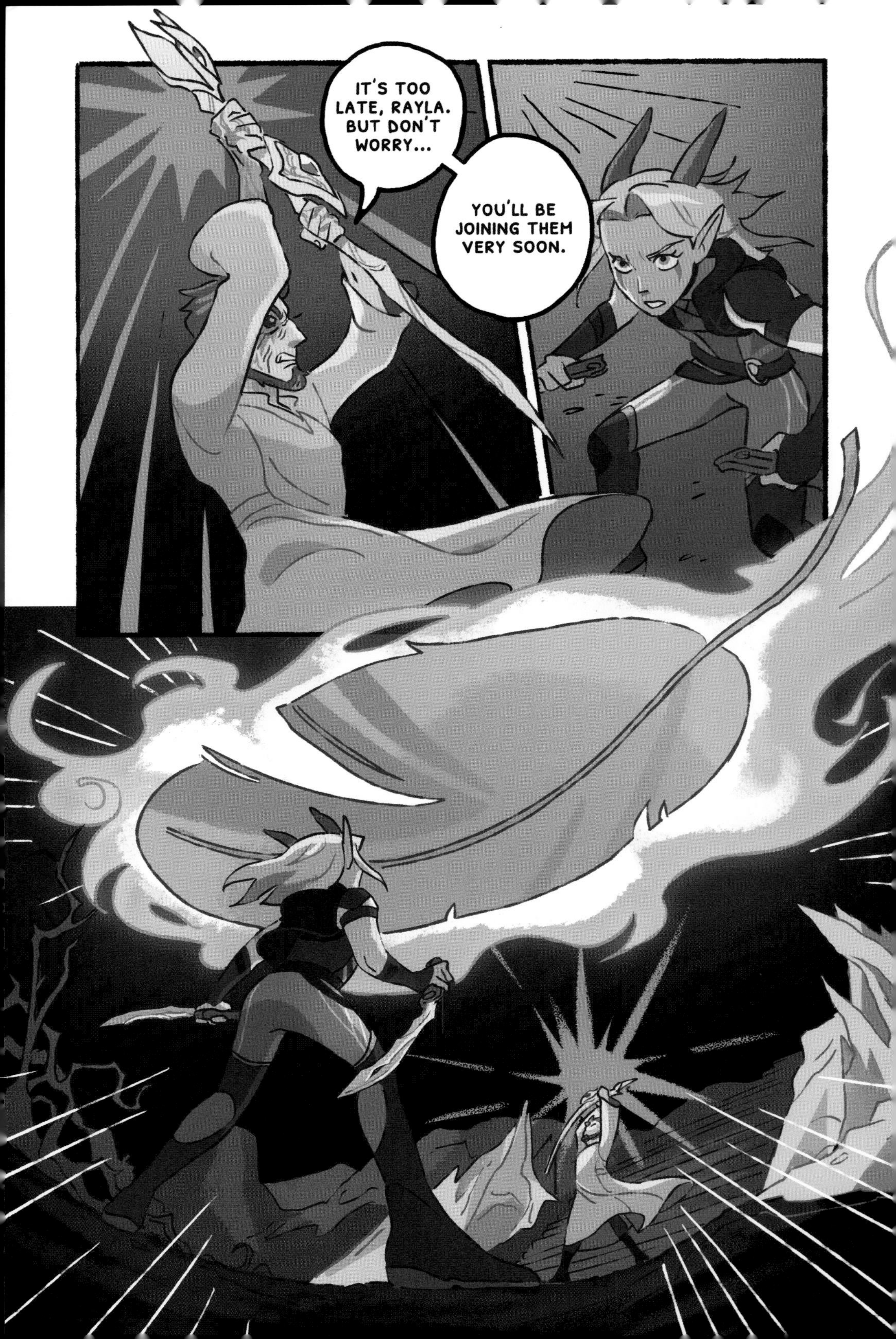
IT'S TOO LATE, RAYLA. BUT DON'T WORRY...
YOU'LL BE JOINING THEM VERY SOON.

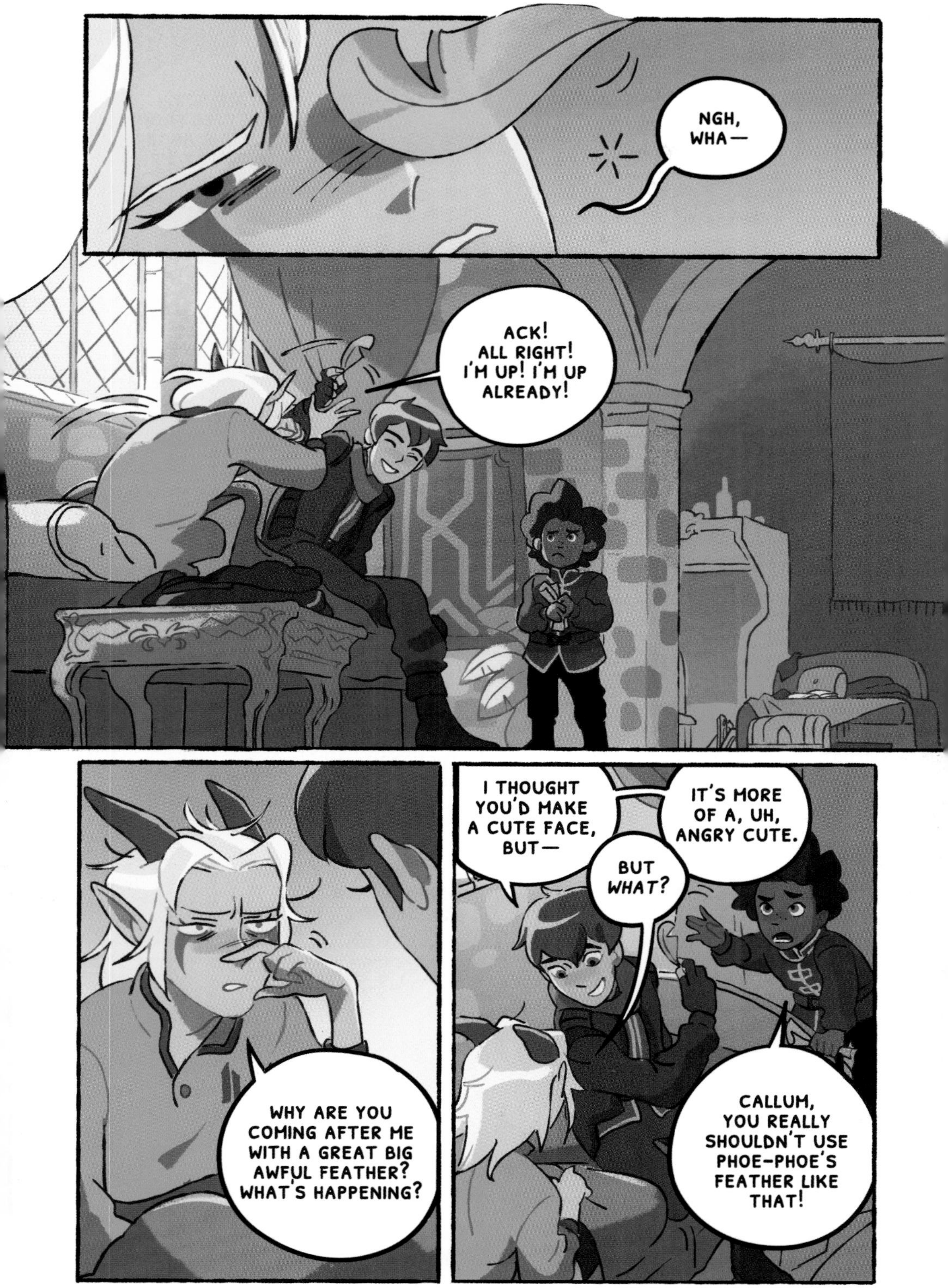
NGH, WHA—
ACK! ALL RIGHT! I'M UP! I'M UP ALREADY!
WHY ARE YOU COMING AFTER ME WITH A GREAT BIG AWFUL FEATHER? WHAT'S HAPPENING?
I THOUGHT YOU'D MAKE A CUTE FACE, BUT—
BUT WHAT?
IT'S MORE OF A, UH, ANGRY CUTE.
CALLUM, YOU REALLY SHOULDN'T USE PHOE-PHOE'S FEATHER LIKE THAT!

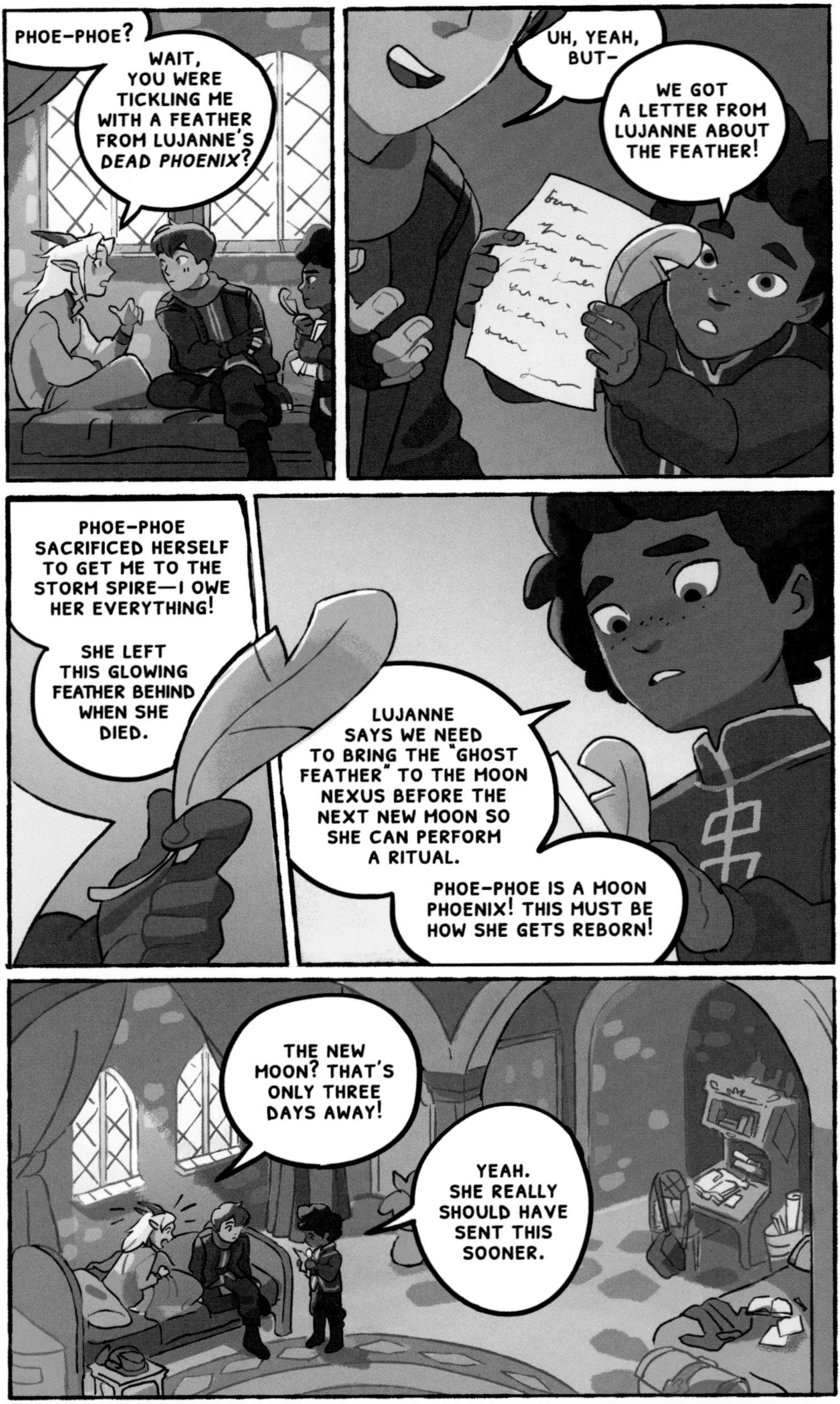
PHOE-PHOE?
WAIT, YOU WERE TICKLING ME WITH A FEATHER FROM LUJANNE'S *DEAD PHOENIX*?
UH, YEAH, BUT–
WE GOT A LETTER FROM LUJANNE ABOUT THE FEATHER!
PHOE-PHOE SACRIFICED HERSELF TO GET ME TO THE STORM SPIRE—I OWE HER EVERYTHING!
SHE LEFT THIS GLOWING FEATHER BEHIND WHEN SHE DIED.
LUJANNE SAYS WE NEED TO BRING THE "GHOST FEATHER" TO THE MOON NEXUS BEFORE THE NEXT NEW MOON SO SHE CAN PERFORM A RITUAL.
PHOE-PHOE IS A MOON PHOENIX! THIS MUST BE HOW SHE GETS REBORN!
THE NEW MOON? THAT'S ONLY THREE DAYS AWAY!
YEAH. SHE REALLY SHOULD HAVE SENT THIS SOONER.

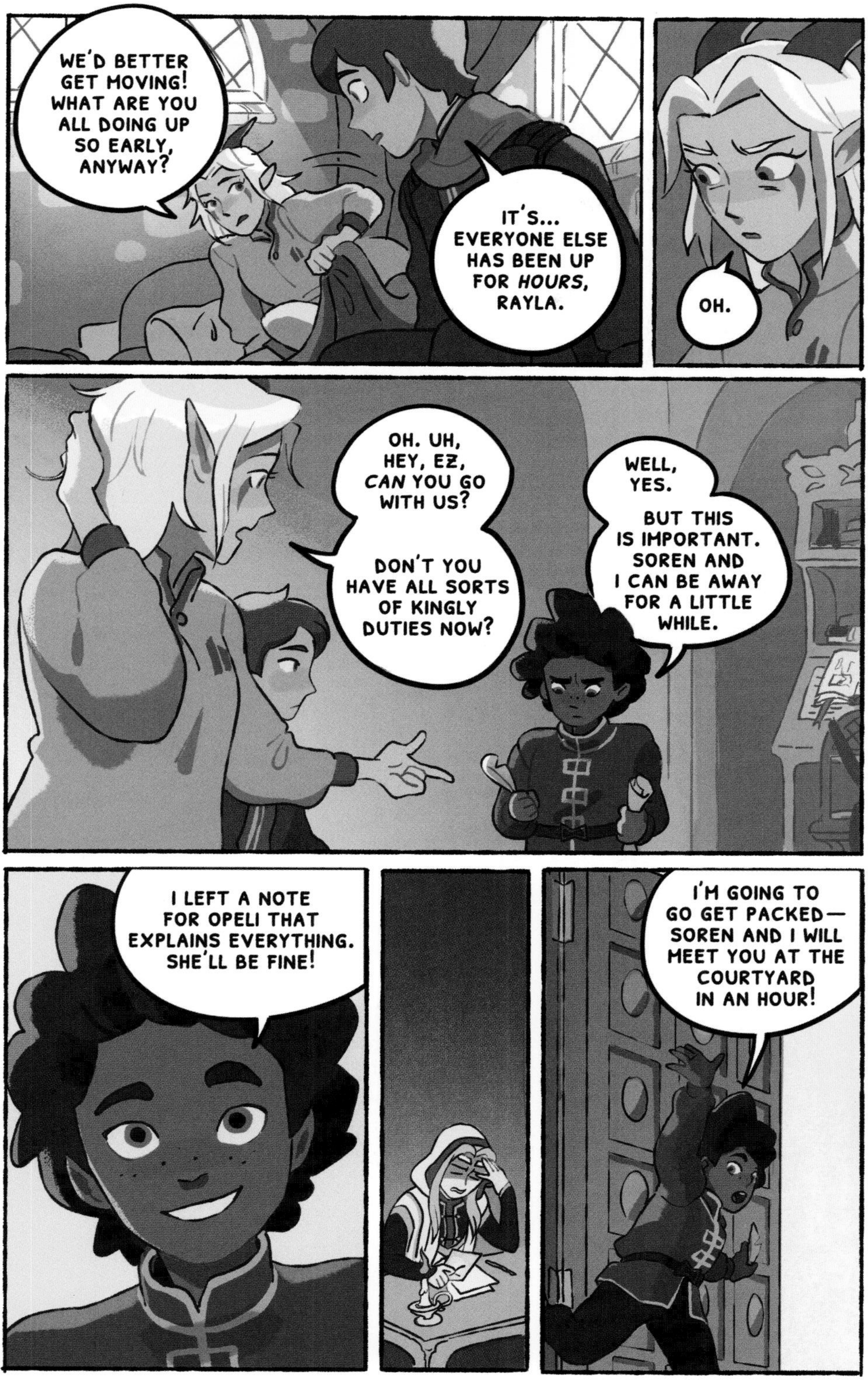
WE'D BETTER GET MOVING! WHAT ARE YOU ALL DOING UP SO EARLY, ANYWAY?
IT'S... EVERYONE ELSE HAS BEEN UP FOR *HOURS*, RAYLA.
OH.
OH. UH, HEY, EZ, *CAN* YOU GO WITH US?
DON'T YOU HAVE ALL SORTS OF KINGLY DUTIES NOW?
WELL, YES.
BUT THIS IS IMPORTANT. SOREN AND I CAN BE AWAY FOR A LITTLE WHILE.
I LEFT A NOTE FOR OPELI THAT EXPLAINS EVERYTHING. SHE'LL BE FINE!
I'M GOING TO GO GET PACKED— SOREN AND I WILL MEET YOU AT THE COURTYARD IN AN HOUR!

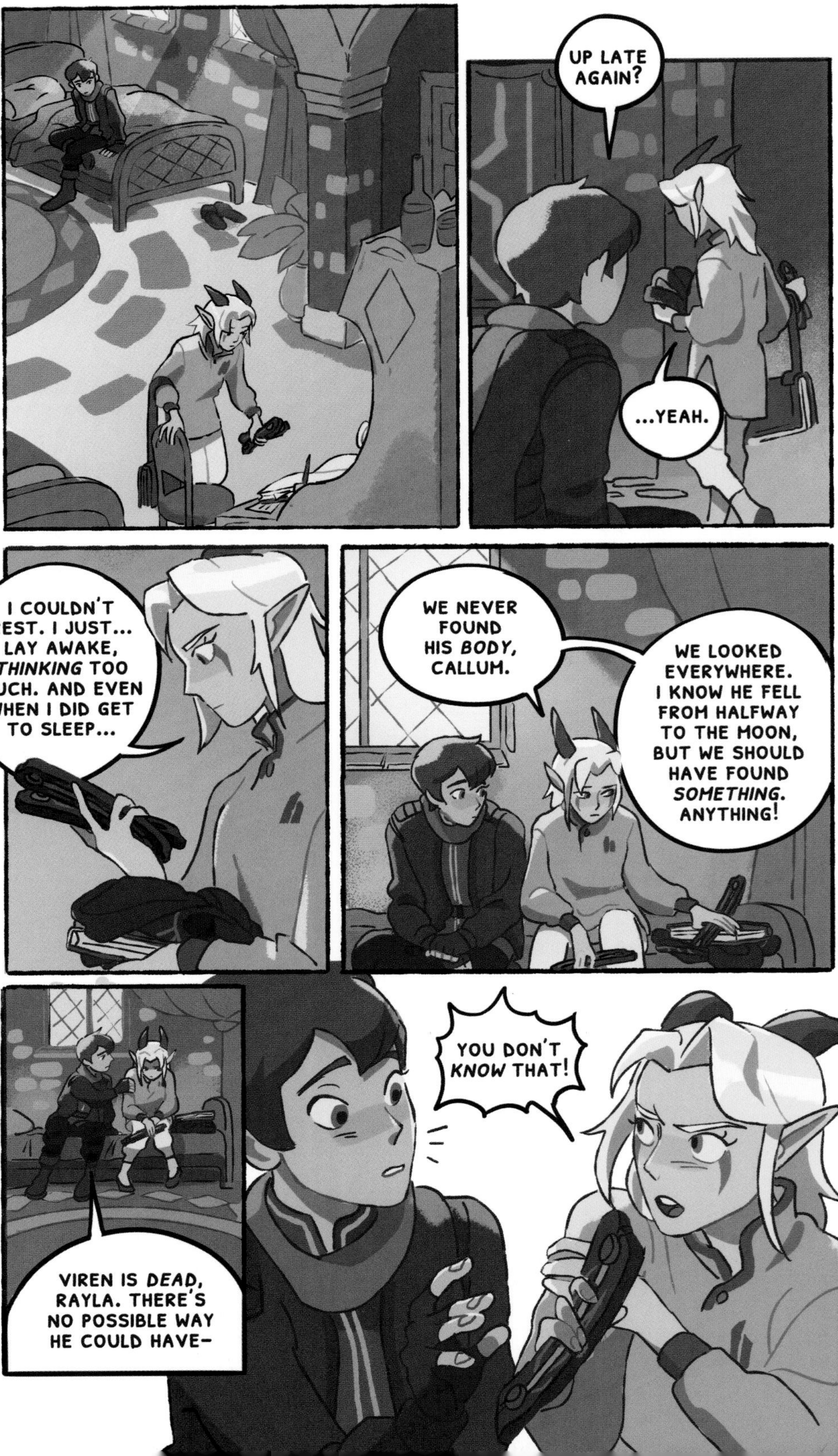
UP LATE AGAIN?
...YEAH.
I COULDN'T REST. I JUST... LAY AWAKE, *THINKING* TOO MUCH. AND EVEN WHEN I DID GET TO SLEEP...
WE NEVER FOUND HIS *BODY*, CALLUM.
WE LOOKED EVERYWHERE. I KNOW HE FELL FROM HALFWAY TO THE MOON, BUT WE SHOULD HAVE FOUND *SOMETHING*. ANYTHING!
VIREN IS *DEAD*, RAYLA. THERE'S NO POSSIBLE WAY HE COULD HAVE-
YOU DON'T *KNOW* THAT!

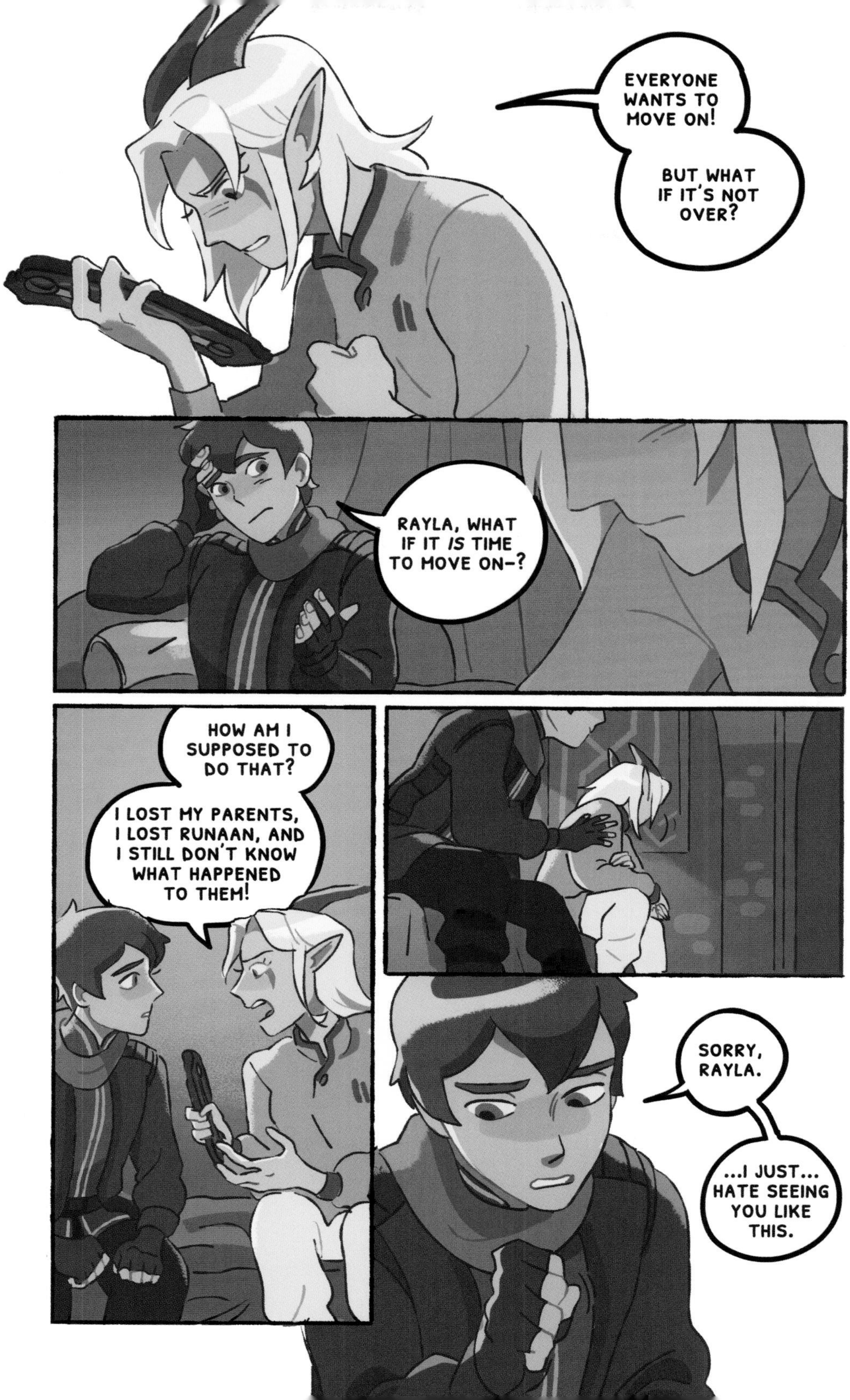
EVERYONE WANTS TO MOVE ON!
BUT WHAT IF IT'S NOT OVER?
RAYLA, WHAT IF IT *IS* TIME TO MOVE ON–?
HOW AM I SUPPOSED TO DO THAT?
I LOST MY PARENTS, I LOST RUNAAN, AND I STILL DON'T KNOW WHAT HAPPENED TO THEM!
SORRY, RAYLA.
...I JUST... HATE SEEING YOU LIKE THIS.

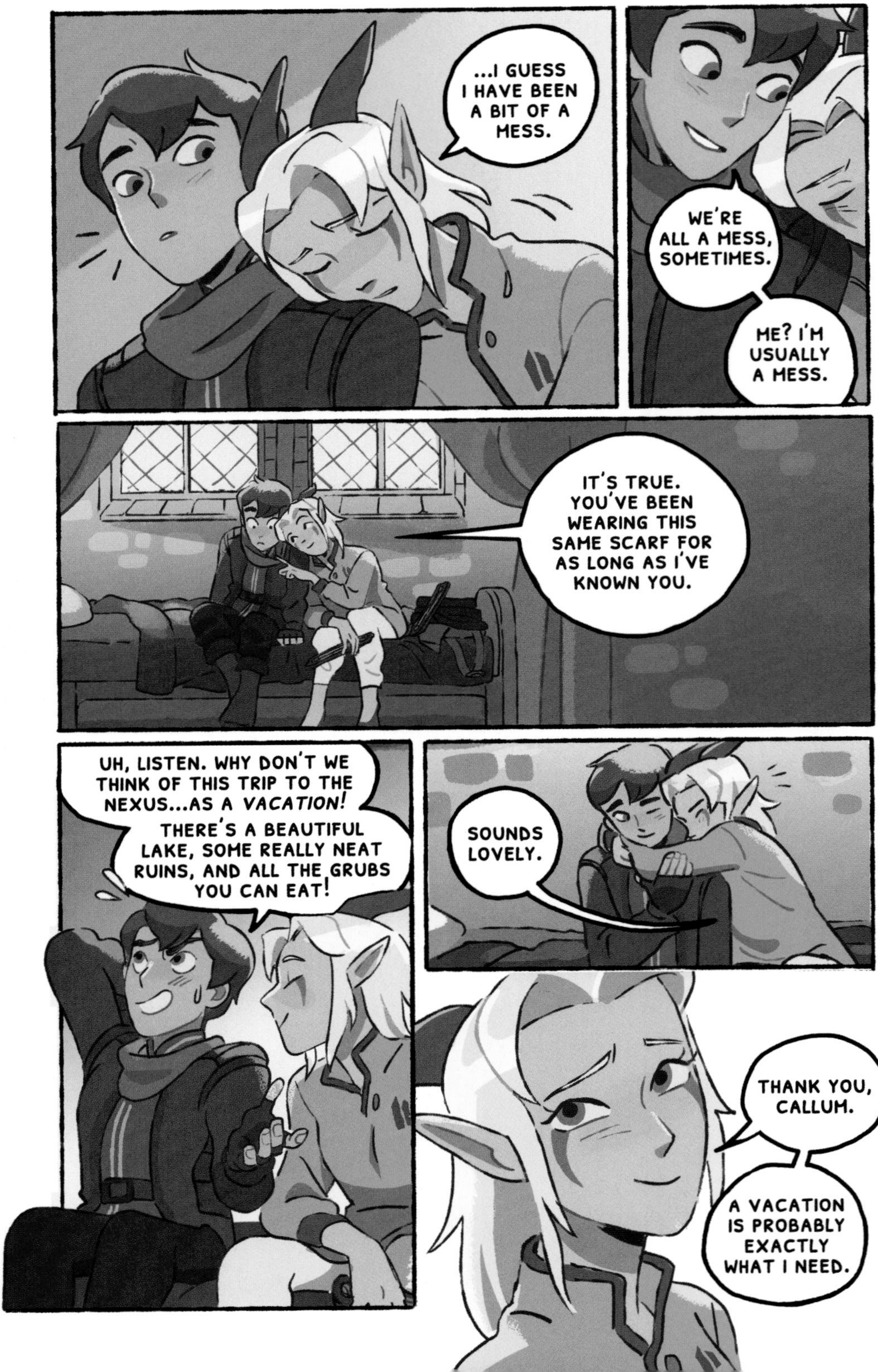
...I GUESS I HAVE BEEN A BIT OF A MESS.
WE'RE ALL A MESS, SOMETIMES.
ME? I'M USUALLY A MESS.
IT'S TRUE. YOU'VE BEEN WEARING THIS SAME SCARF FOR AS LONG AS I'VE KNOWN YOU.
UH, LISTEN. WHY DON'T WE THINK OF THIS TRIP TO THE NEXUS...AS A *VACATION*!
THERE'S A BEAUTIFUL LAKE, SOME REALLY NEAT RUINS, AND ALL THE GRUBS YOU CAN EAT!
SOUNDS LOVELY.
THANK YOU, CALLUM.
A VACATION IS PROBABLY EXACTLY WHAT I NEED.

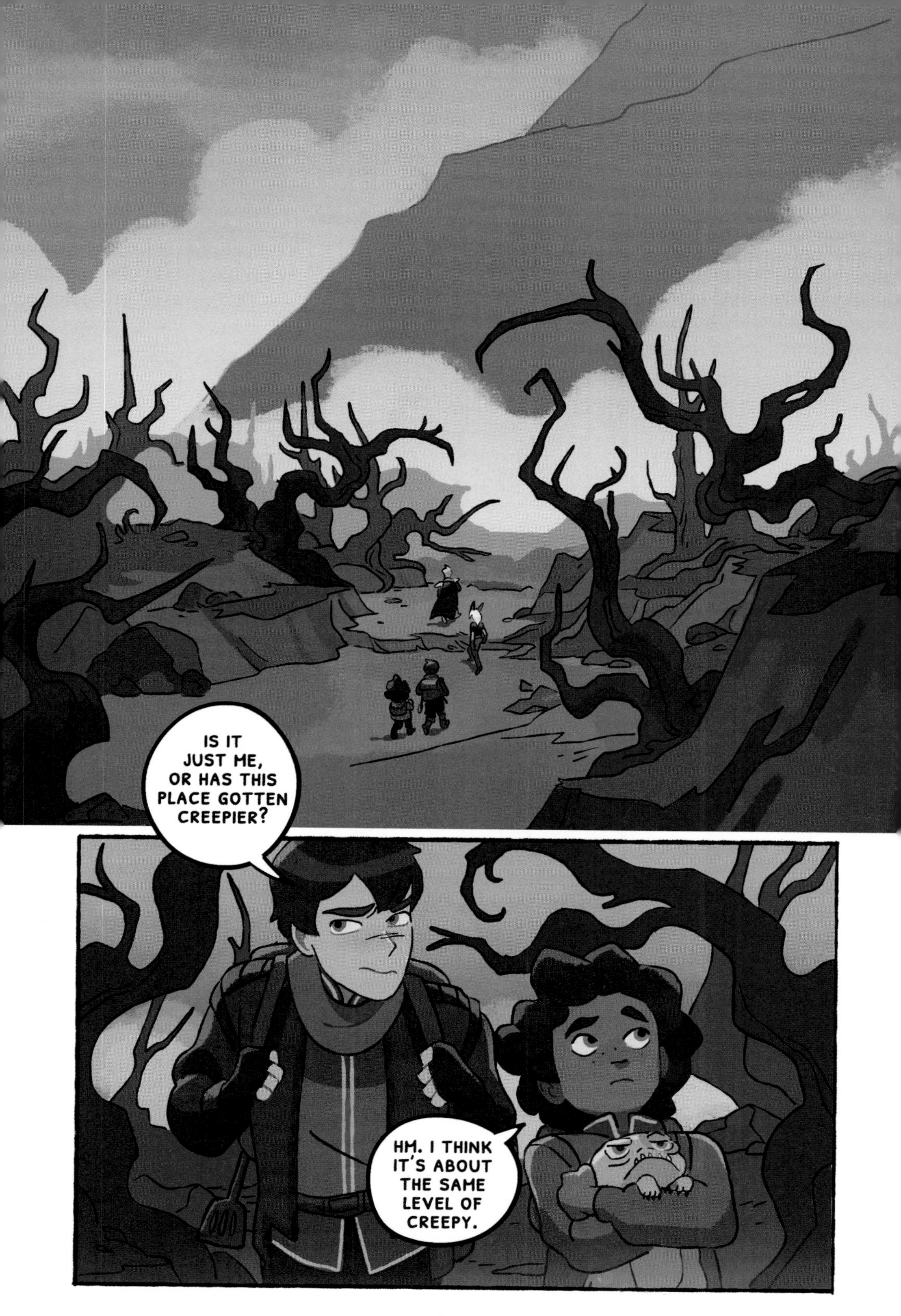
IS IT JUST ME, OR HAS THIS PLACE GOTTEN CREEPIER?
HM. I THINK IT'S ABOUT THE SAME LEVEL OF CREEPY.

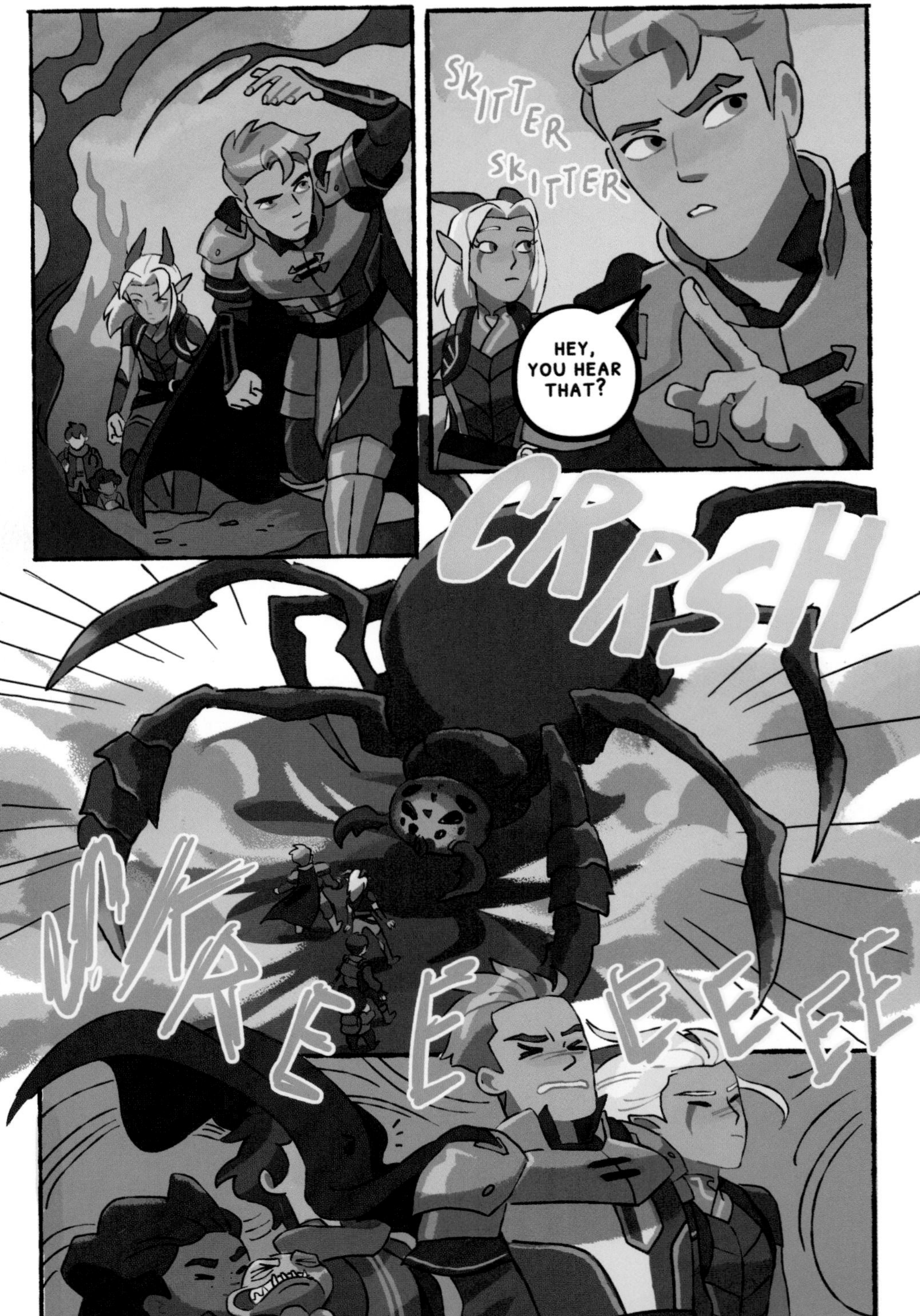
SKITTER SKITTER
HEY, YOU HEAR THAT?
CRRSH
VKREEEEEEE

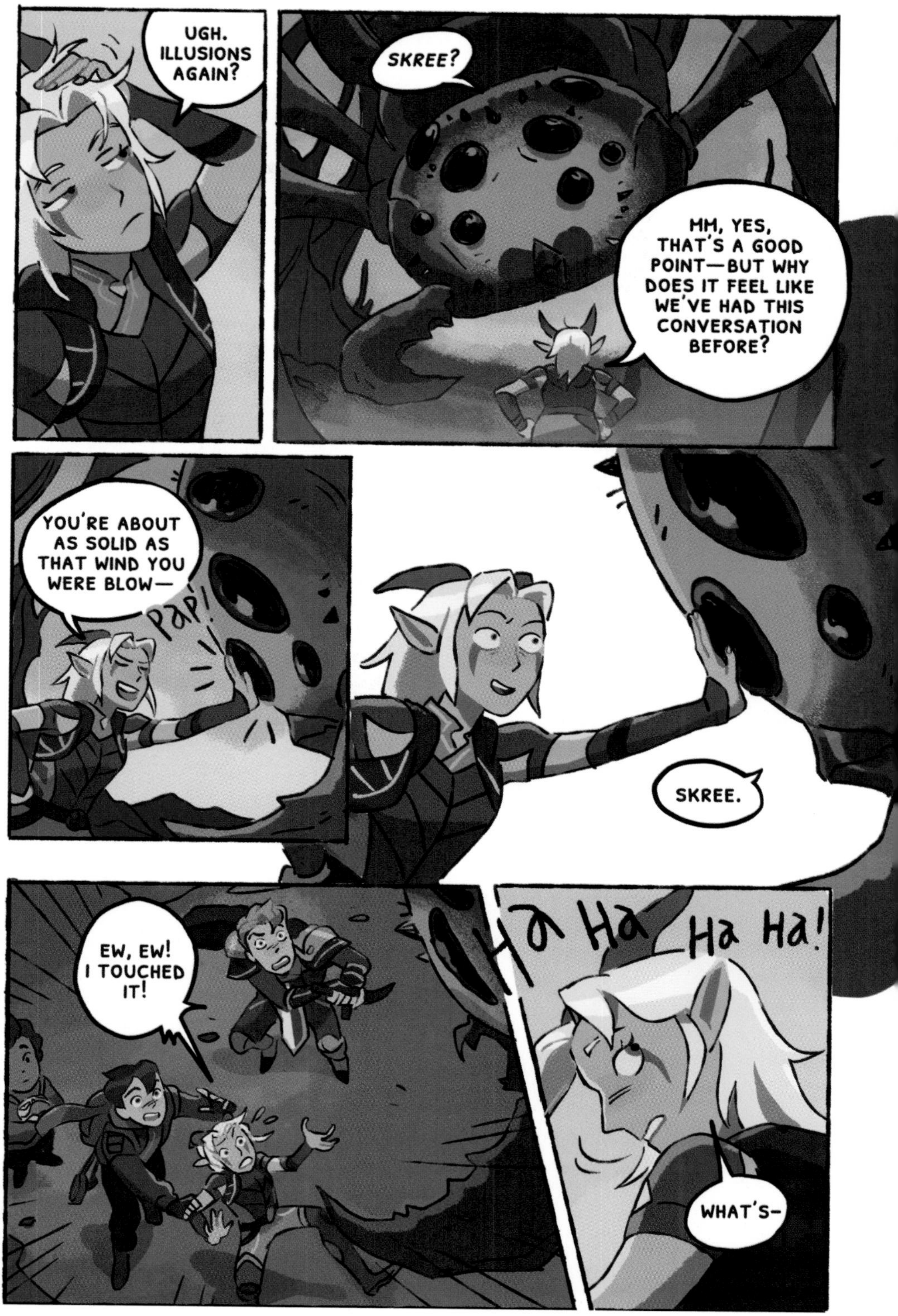
UGH. ILLUSIONS AGAIN?
SKREE?
MM, YES, THAT'S A GOOD POINT—BUT WHY DOES IT FEEL LIKE WE'VE HAD THIS CONVERSATION BEFORE?
YOU'RE ABOUT AS SOLID AS THAT WIND YOU WERE BLOW—
PAP!
SKREE.
EW, EW! I TOUCHED IT!
Ha Ha Ha Ha!
WHAT'S-

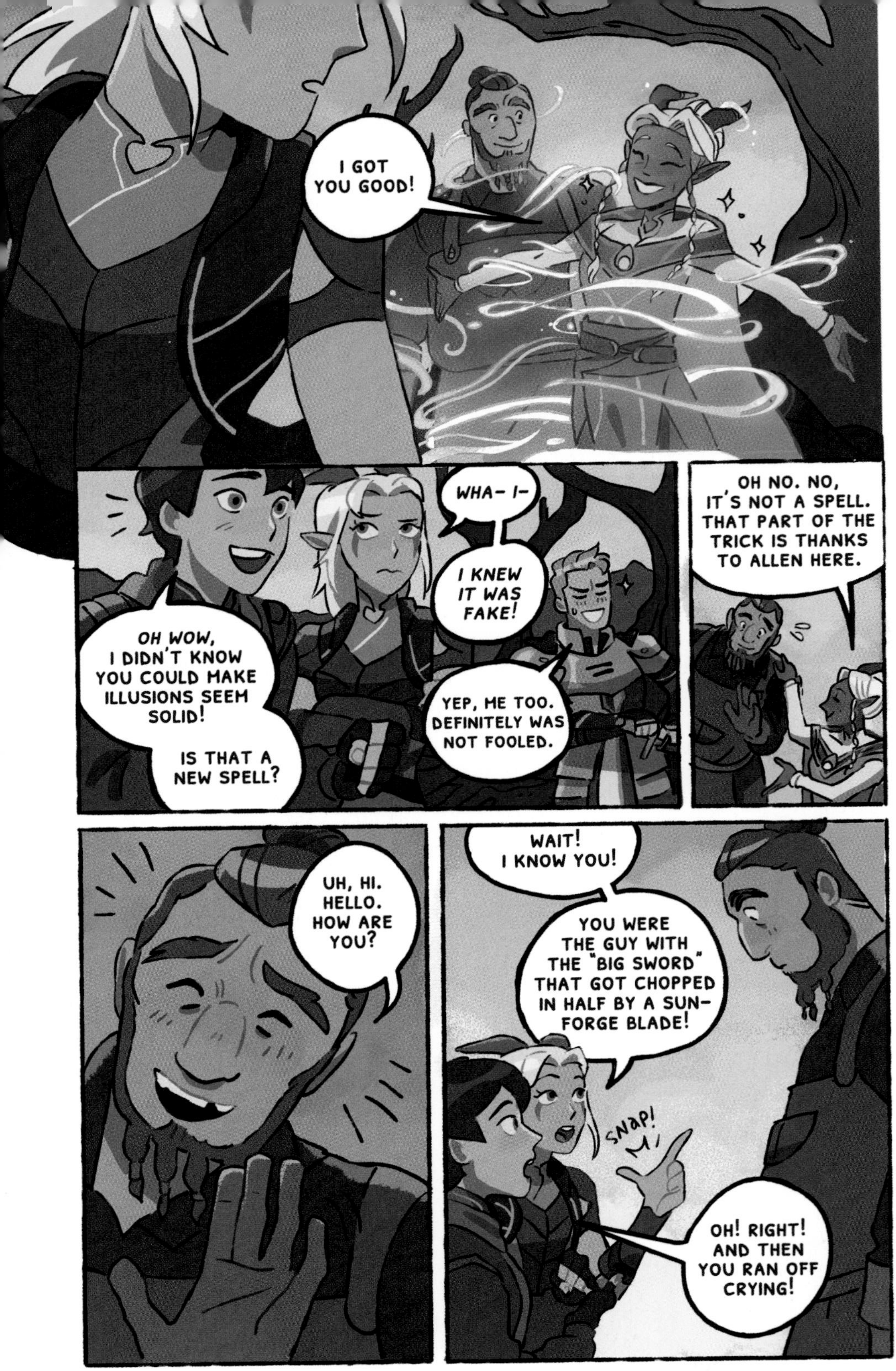
I GOT YOU GOOD!
WHA- I-
I KNEW IT WAS FAKE!
OH WOW, I DIDN'T KNOW YOU COULD MAKE ILLUSIONS SEEM SOLID!
IS THAT A NEW SPELL?
YEP, ME TOO. DEFINITELY WAS NOT FOOLED.
OH NO. NO, IT'S NOT A SPELL. THAT PART OF THE TRICK IS THANKS TO ALLEN HERE.
UH, HI. HELLO. HOW ARE YOU?
WAIT! I KNOW YOU!
YOU WERE THE GUY WITH THE "BIG SWORD" THAT GOT CHOPPED IN HALF BY A SUN-FORGE BLADE!
SNAP!
OH! RIGHT! AND THEN YOU RAN OFF CRYING!

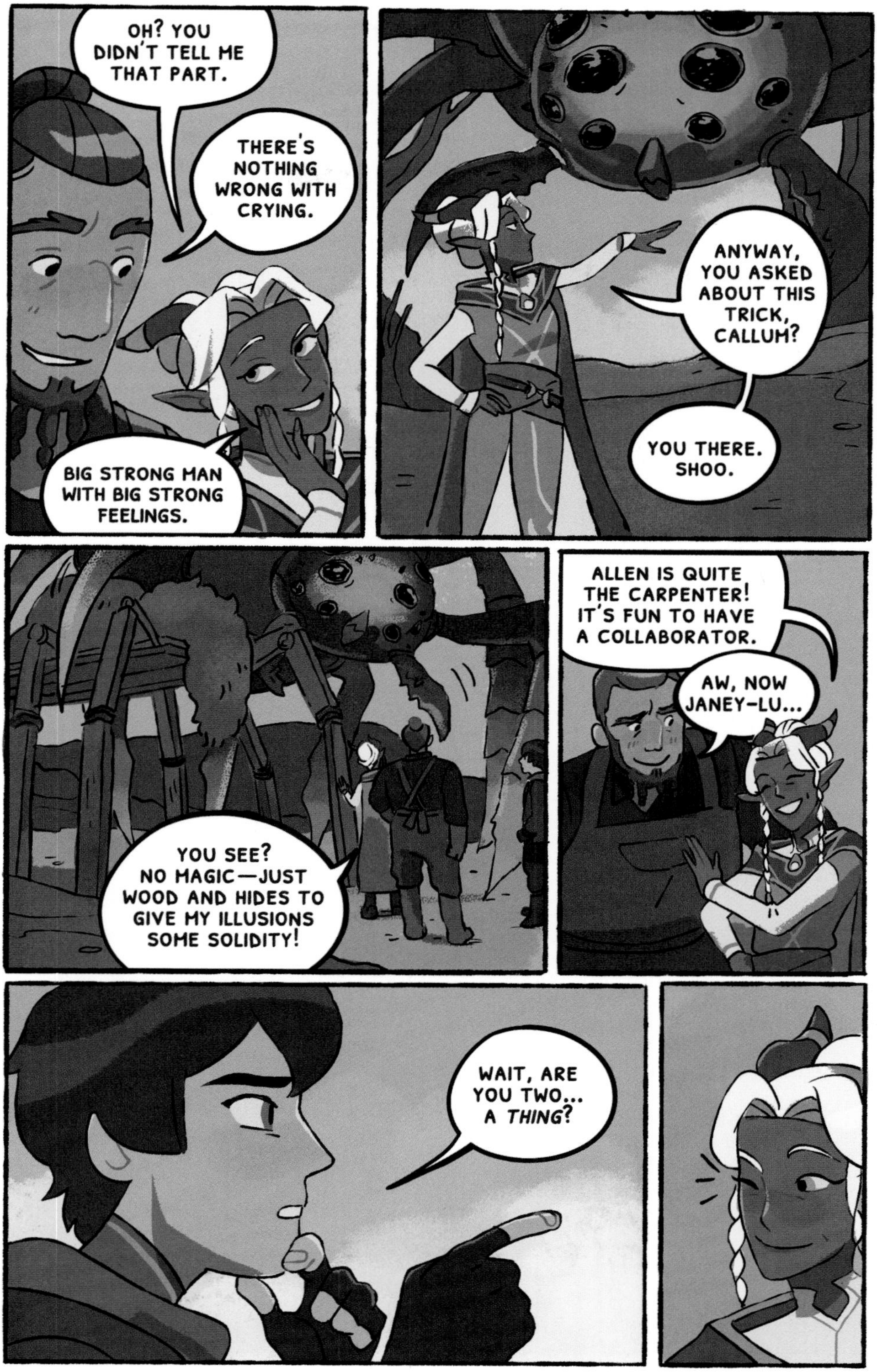
OH? YOU DIDN'T TELL ME THAT PART.
THERE'S NOTHING WRONG WITH CRYING.
BIG STRONG MAN WITH BIG STRONG FEELINGS.
ANYWAY, YOU ASKED ABOUT THIS TRICK, CALLUM?
YOU THERE. SHOO.
YOU SEE? NO MAGIC—JUST WOOD AND HIDES TO GIVE MY ILLUSIONS SOME SOLIDITY!
ALLEN IS QUITE THE CARPENTER! IT'S FUN TO HAVE A COLLABORATOR.
AW, NOW JANEY-LU...
WAIT, ARE YOU TWO... A *THING*?

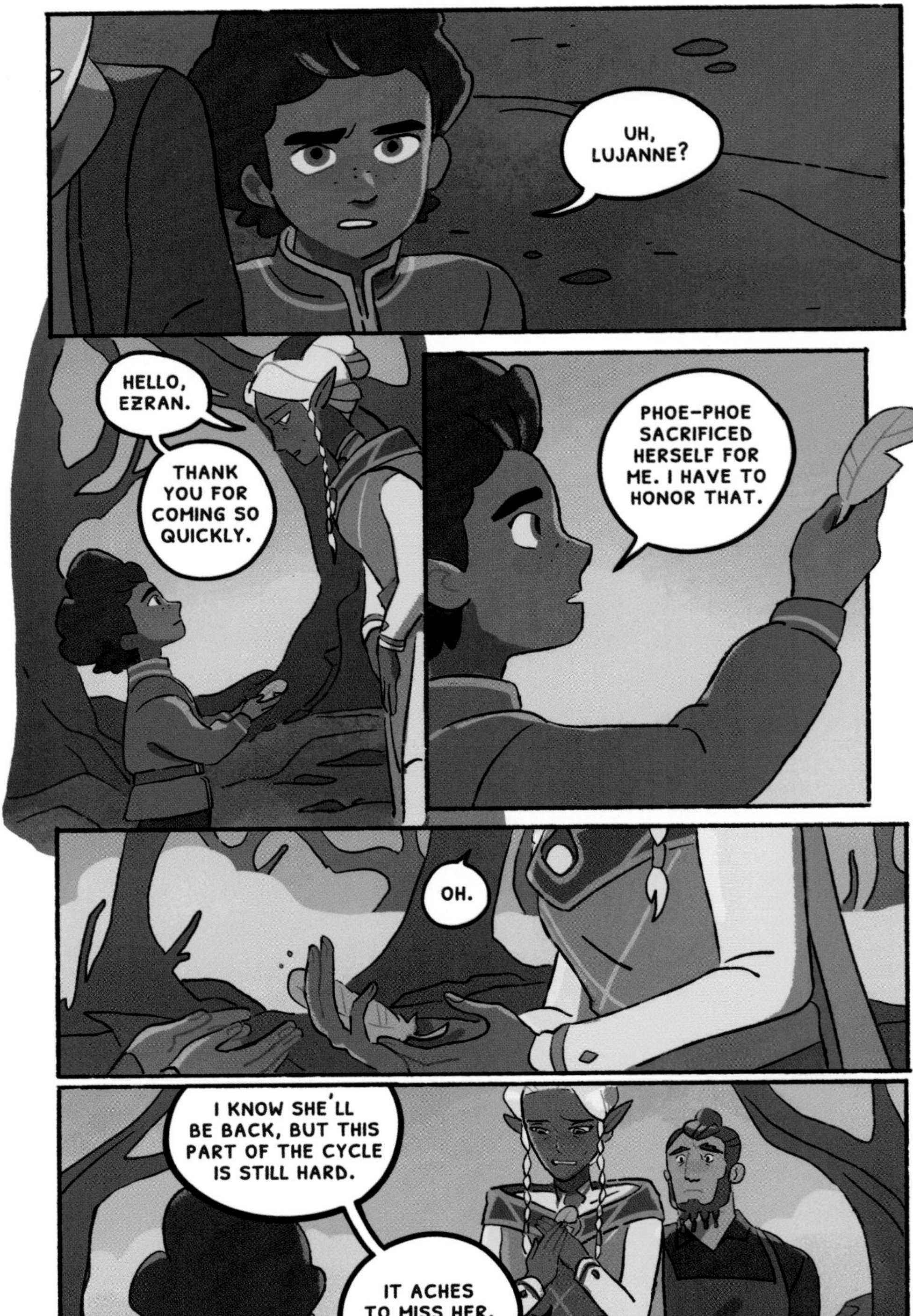
UH, LUJANNE?
HELLO, EZRAN.
THANK YOU FOR COMING SO QUICKLY.
PHOE-PHOE SACRIFICED HERSELF FOR ME. I HAVE TO HONOR THAT.
OH.
I KNOW SHE'LL BE BACK, BUT THIS PART OF THE CYCLE IS STILL HARD.
IT ACHES TO MISS HER.

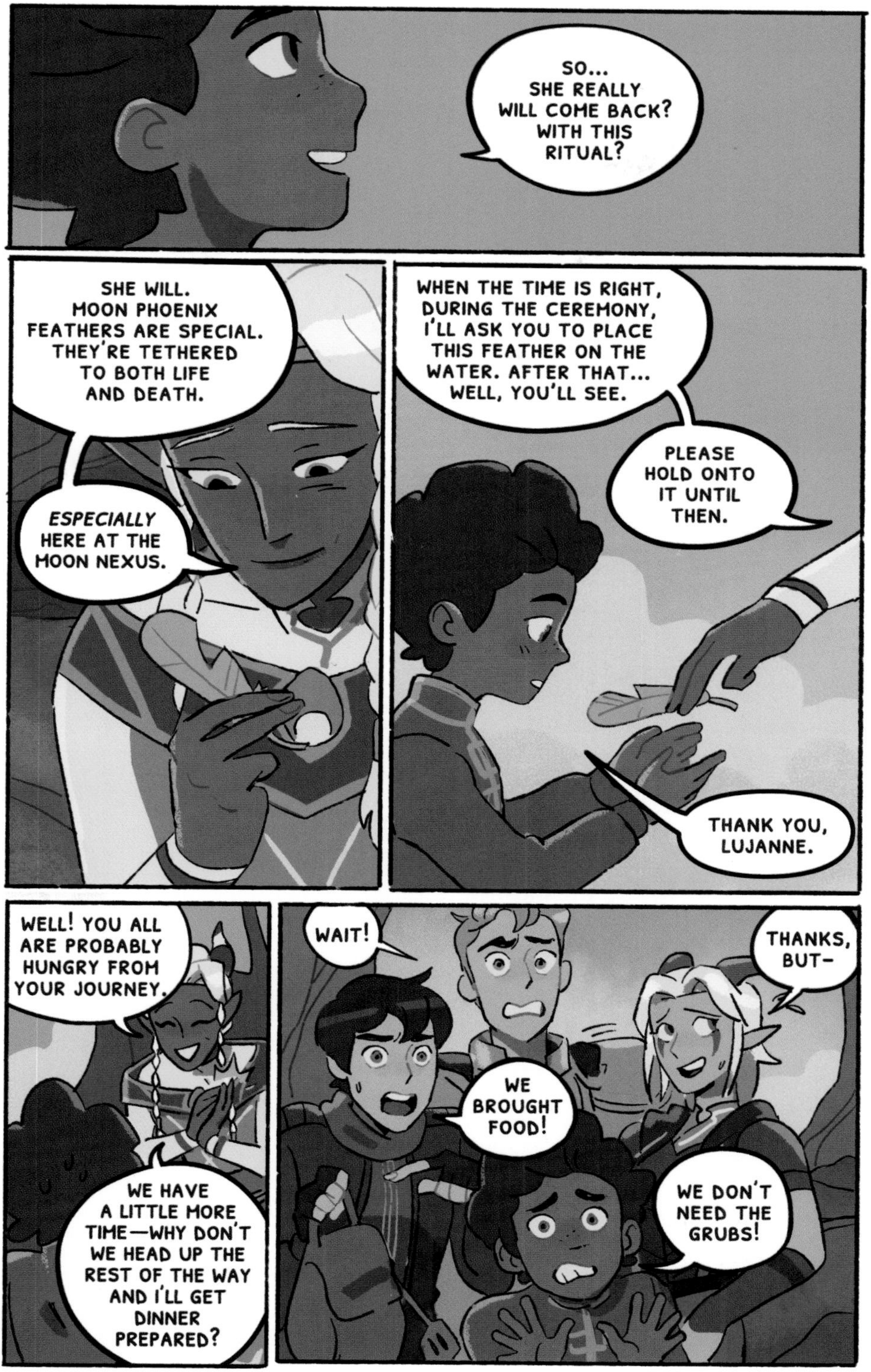
SO... SHE REALLY WILL COME BACK? WITH THIS RITUAL?
SHE WILL. MOON PHOENIX FEATHERS ARE SPECIAL. THEY'RE TETHERED TO BOTH LIFE AND DEATH.
ESPECIALLY HERE AT THE MOON NEXUS.
WHEN THE TIME IS RIGHT, DURING THE CEREMONY, I'LL ASK YOU TO PLACE THIS FEATHER ON THE WATER. AFTER THAT... WELL, YOU'LL SEE.
PLEASE HOLD ONTO IT UNTIL THEN.
THANK YOU, LUJANNE.
WELL! YOU ALL ARE PROBABLY HUNGRY FROM YOUR JOURNEY.
WE HAVE A LITTLE MORE TIME—WHY DON'T WE HEAD UP THE REST OF THE WAY AND I'LL GET DINNER PREPARED?
WAIT!
THANKS, BUT-
WE BROUGHT FOOD!
WE DON'T NEED THE GRUBS!

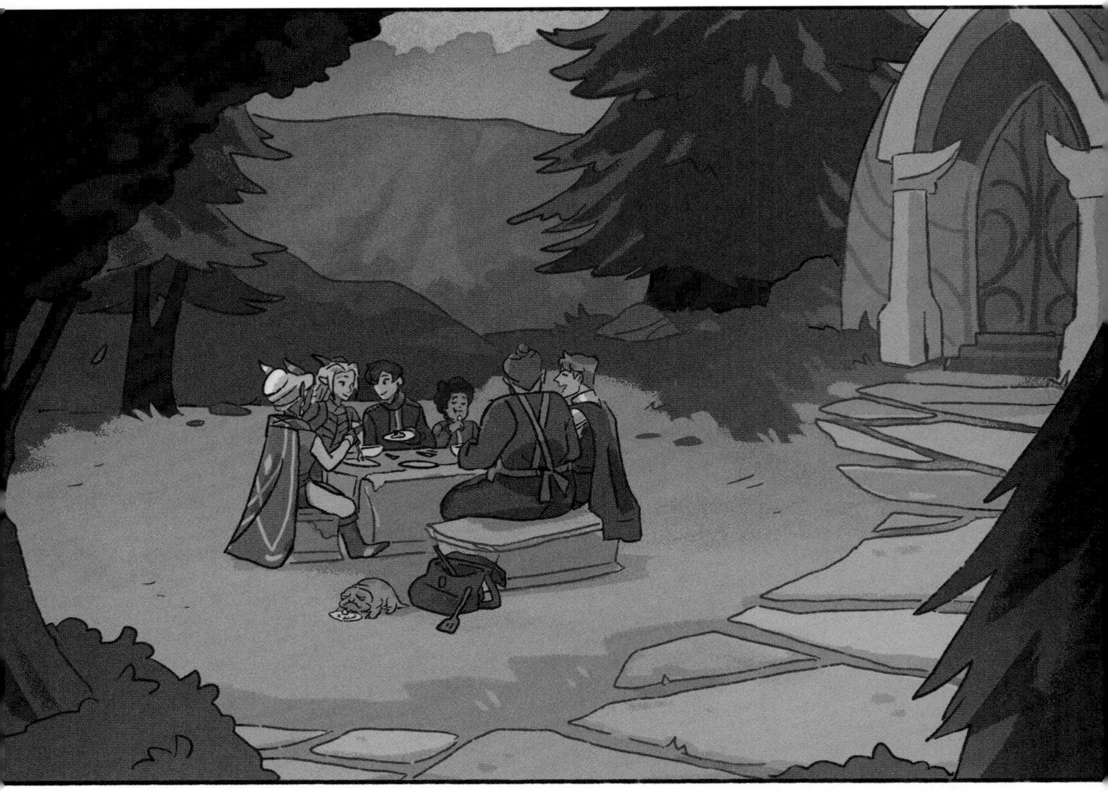

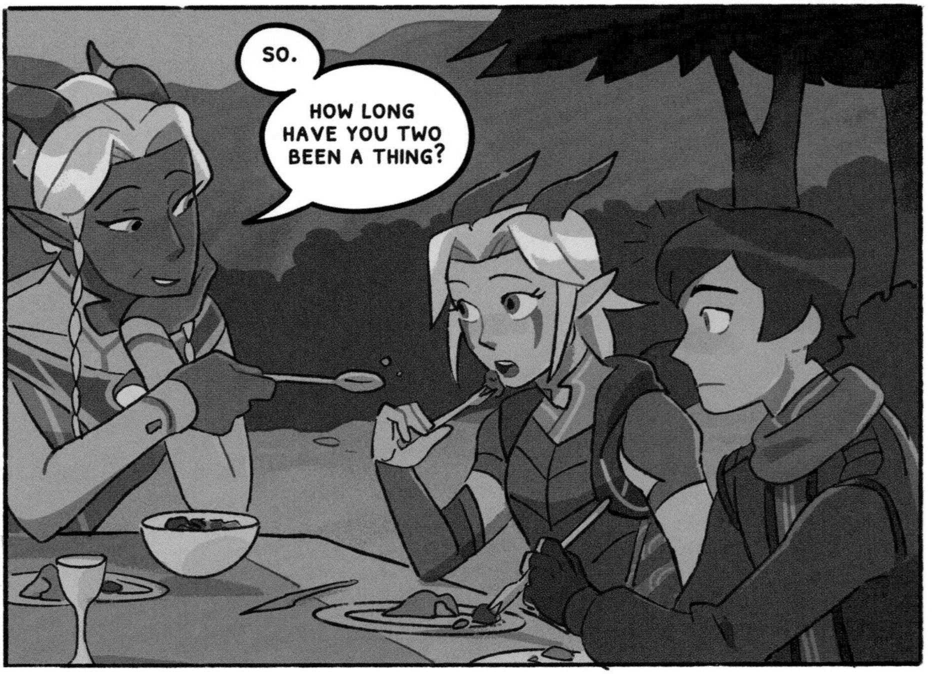
SO.
HOW LONG HAVE YOU TWO BEEN A THING?

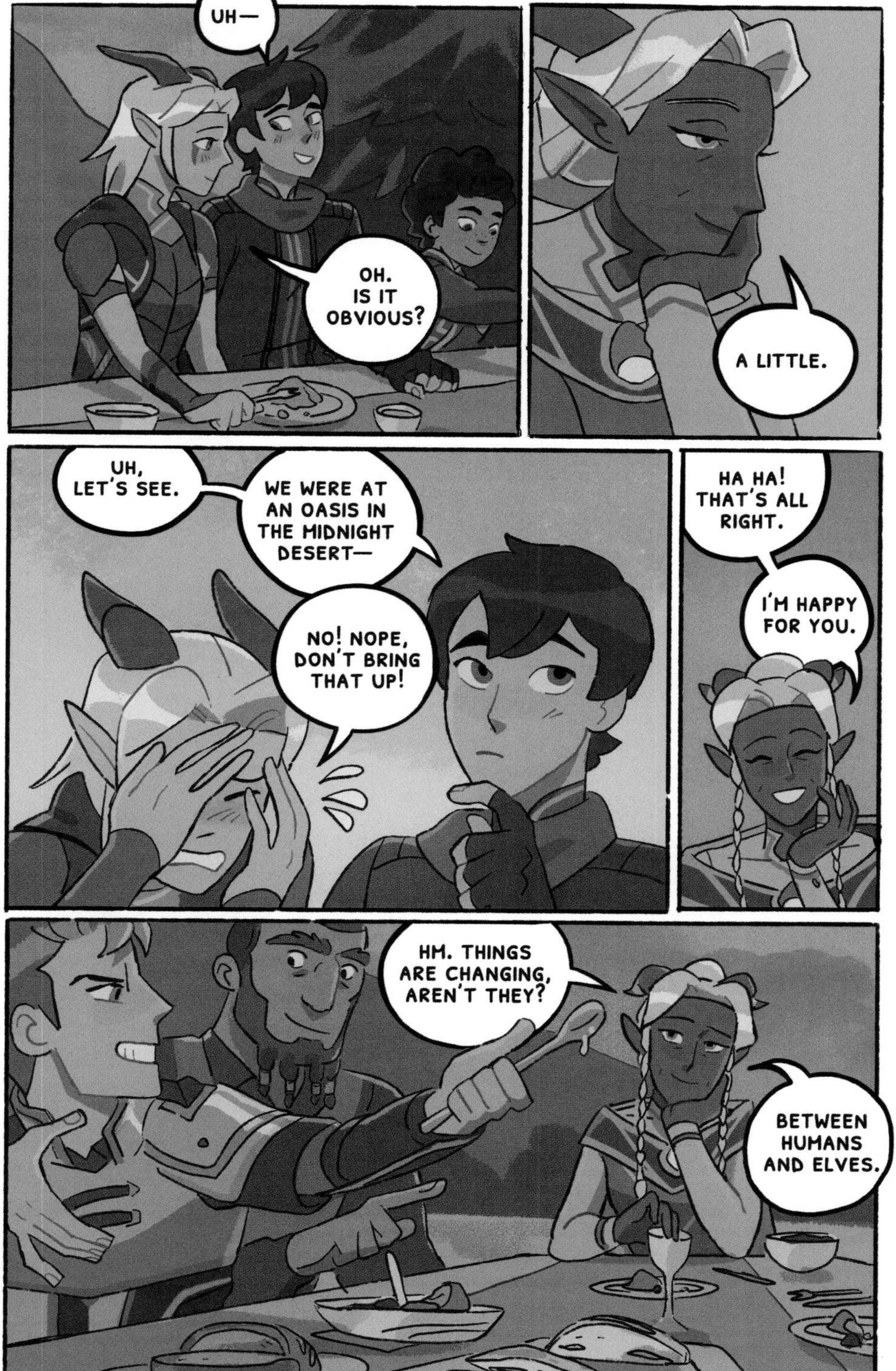
UH—
OH. IS IT OBVIOUS?
A LITTLE.
UH, LET'S SEE.
WE WERE AT AN OASIS IN THE MIDNIGHT DESERT—
NO! NOPE, DON'T BRING THAT UP!
HA HA! THAT'S ALL RIGHT.
I'M HAPPY FOR YOU.
HM. THINGS ARE CHANGING, AREN'T THEY?
BETWEEN HUMANS AND ELVES.

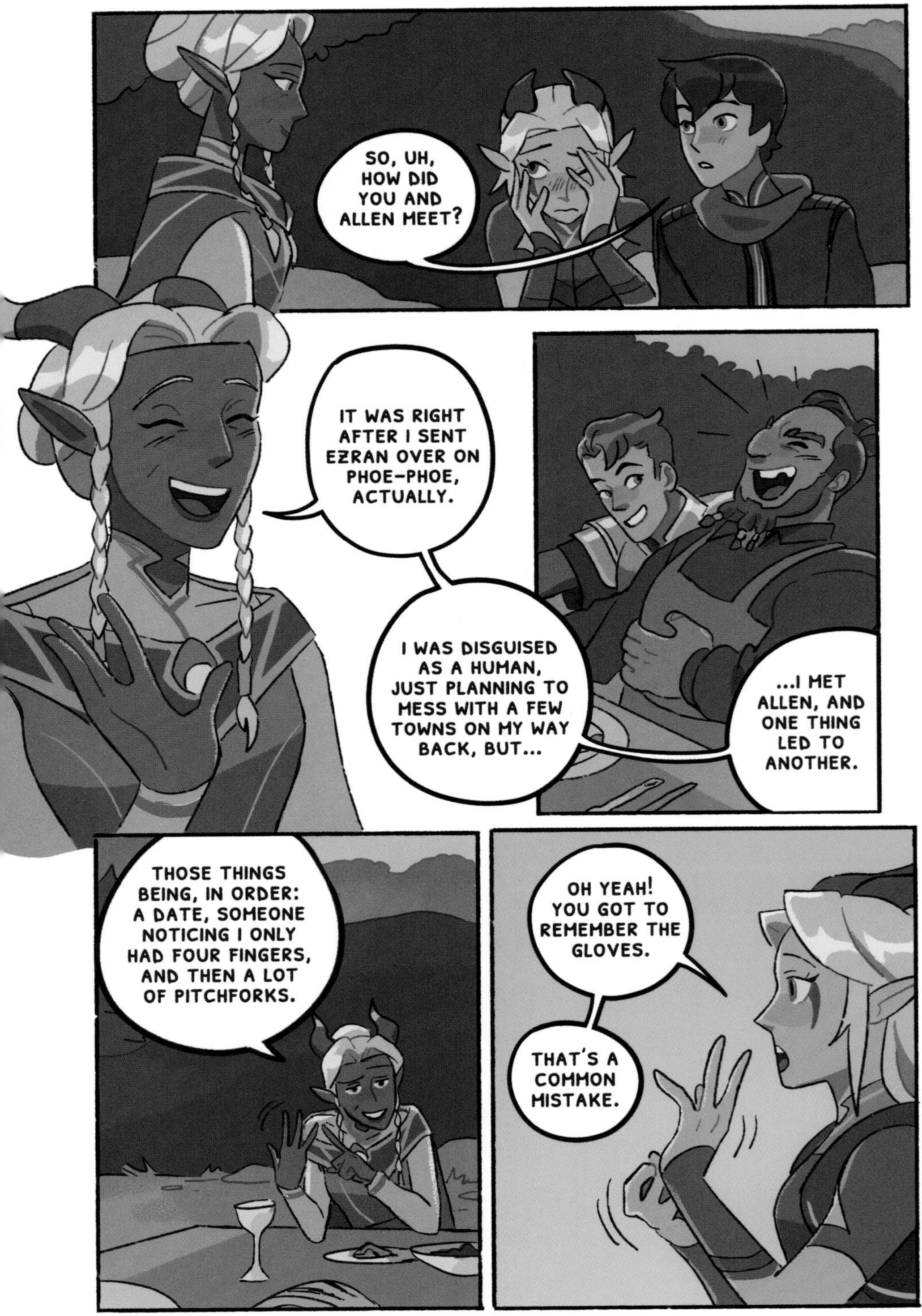
SO, UH, HOW DID YOU AND ALLEN MEET?
IT WAS RIGHT AFTER I SENT EZRAN OVER ON PHOE-PHOE, ACTUALLY.
I WAS DISGUISED AS A HUMAN, JUST PLANNING TO MESS WITH A FEW TOWNS ON MY WAY BACK, BUT...
...I MET ALLEN, AND ONE THING LED TO ANOTHER.
THOSE THINGS BEING, IN ORDER: A DATE, SOMEONE NOTICING I ONLY HAD FOUR FINGERS, AND THEN A LOT OF PITCHFORKS.
OH YEAH! YOU GOT TO REMEMBER THE GLOVES.
THAT'S A COMMON MISTAKE.

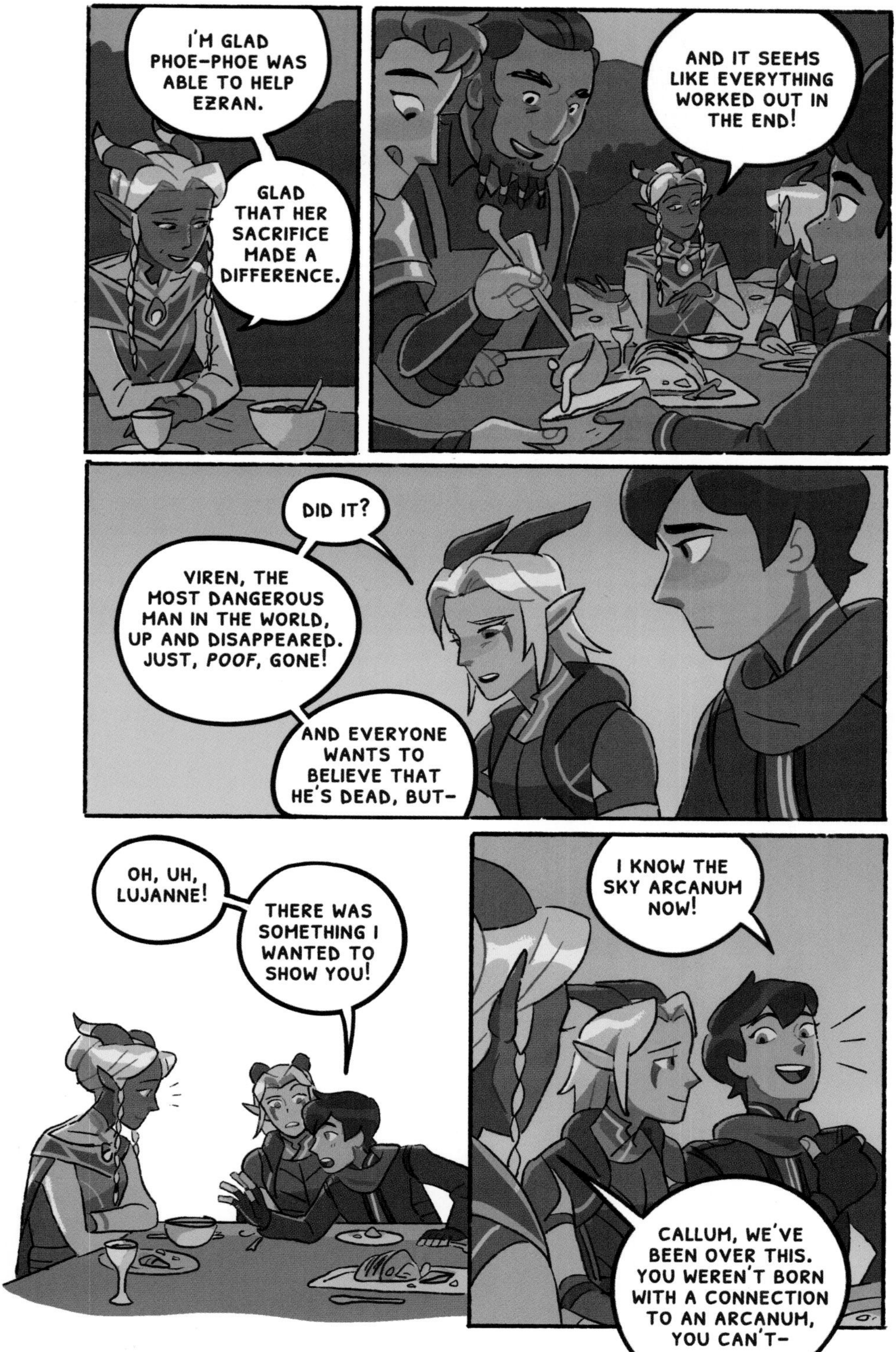
I'M GLAD PHOE-PHOE WAS ABLE TO HELP EZRAN.
GLAD THAT HER SACRIFICE MADE A DIFFERENCE.
AND IT SEEMS LIKE EVERYTHING WORKED OUT IN THE END!
DID IT?
VIREN, THE MOST DANGEROUS MAN IN THE WORLD, UP AND DISAPPEARED. JUST, *POOF*, GONE!
AND EVERYONE WANTS TO BELIEVE THAT HE'S DEAD, BUT-
OH, UH, LUJANNE!
THERE WAS SOMETHING I WANTED TO SHOW YOU!
I KNOW THE SKY ARCANUM NOW!
CALLUM, WE'VE BEEN OVER THIS. YOU WEREN'T BORN WITH A CONNECTION TO AN ARCANUM, YOU CAN'T-

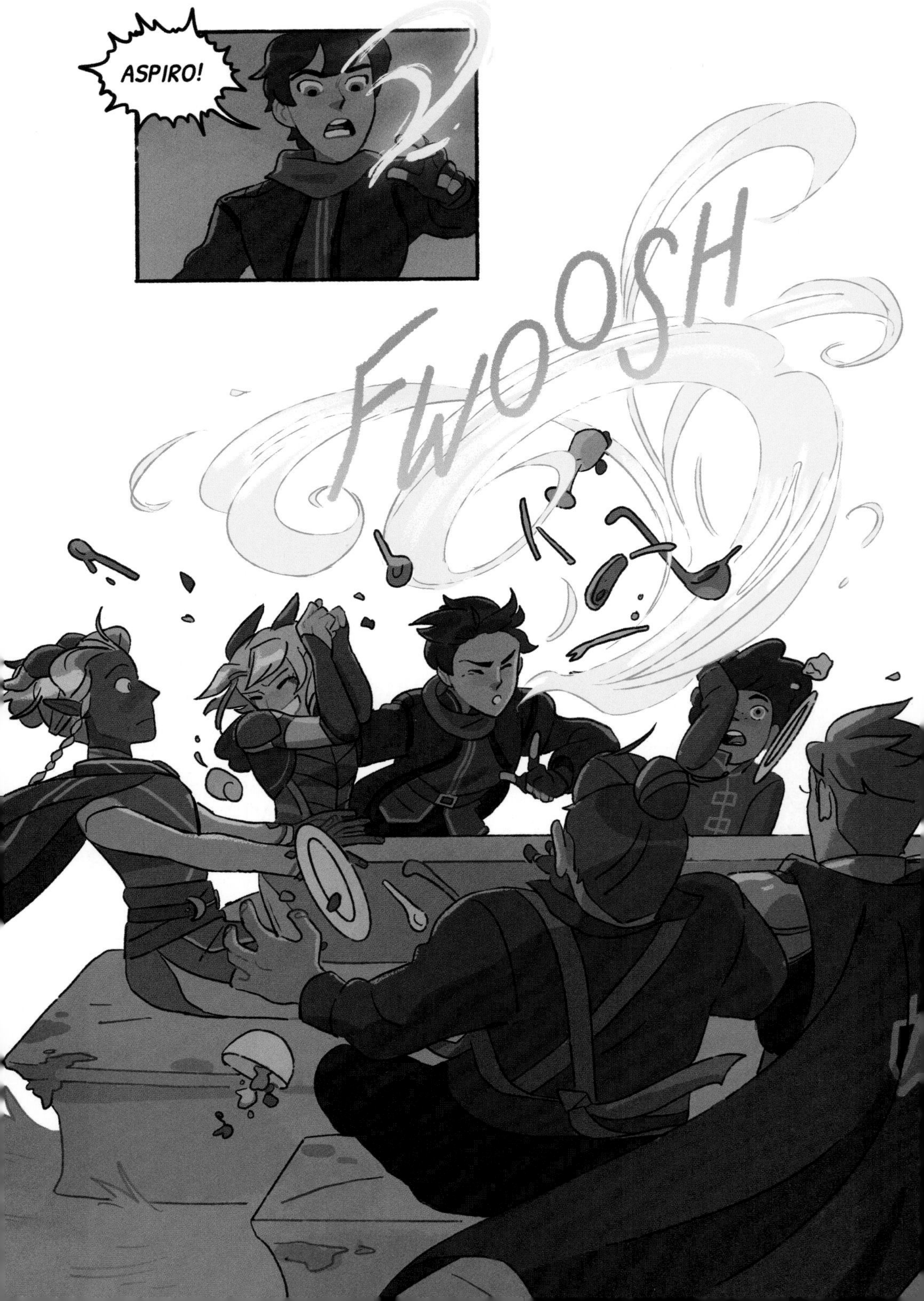
ASPIRO!
FWOOSH

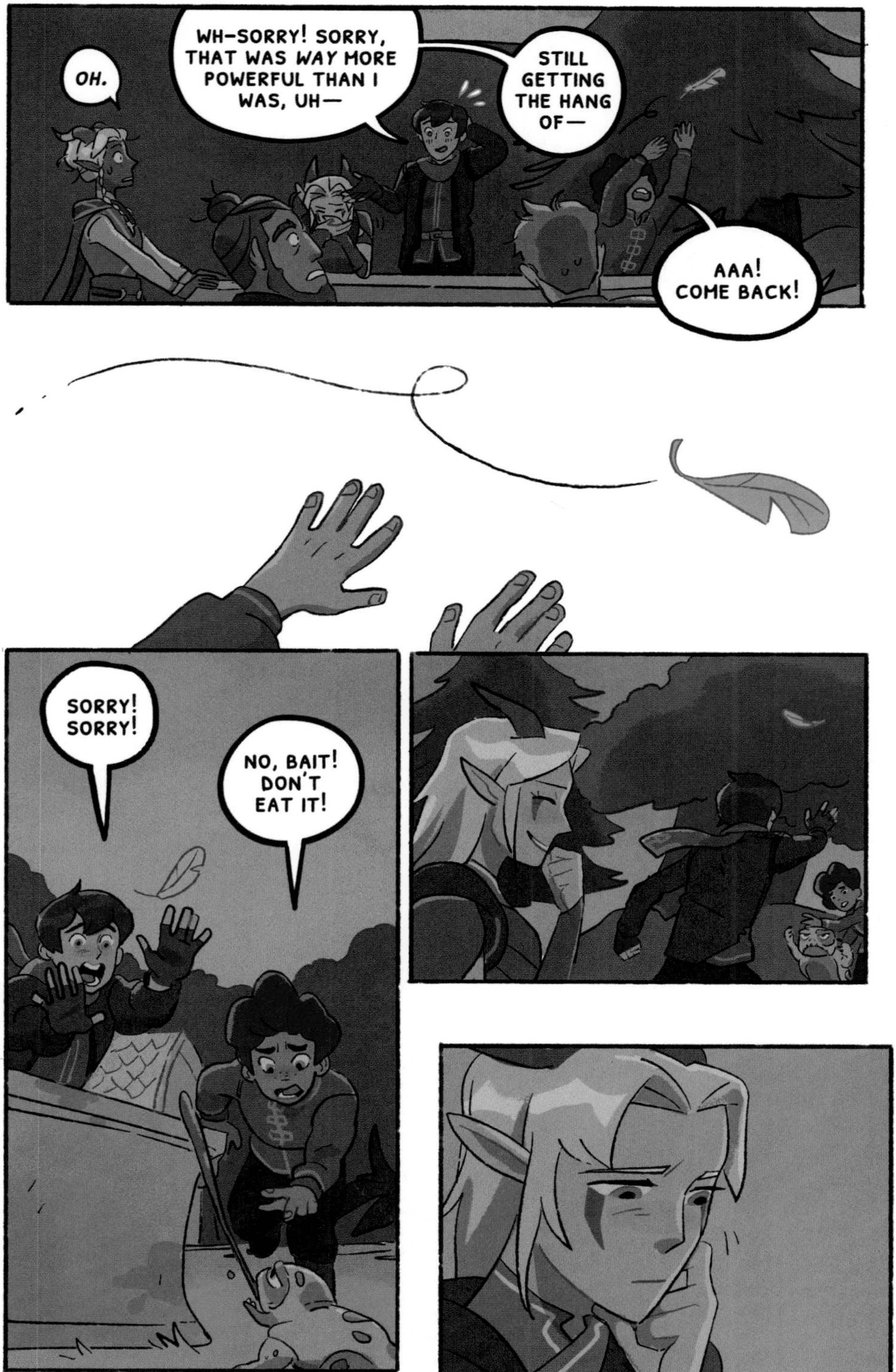
OH.
WH—SORRY! SORRY, THAT WAS WAY MORE POWERFUL THAN I WAS, UH—
STILL GETTING THE HANG OF—
AAA! COME BACK!
SORRY! SORRY!
NO, BAIT! DON'T EAT IT!

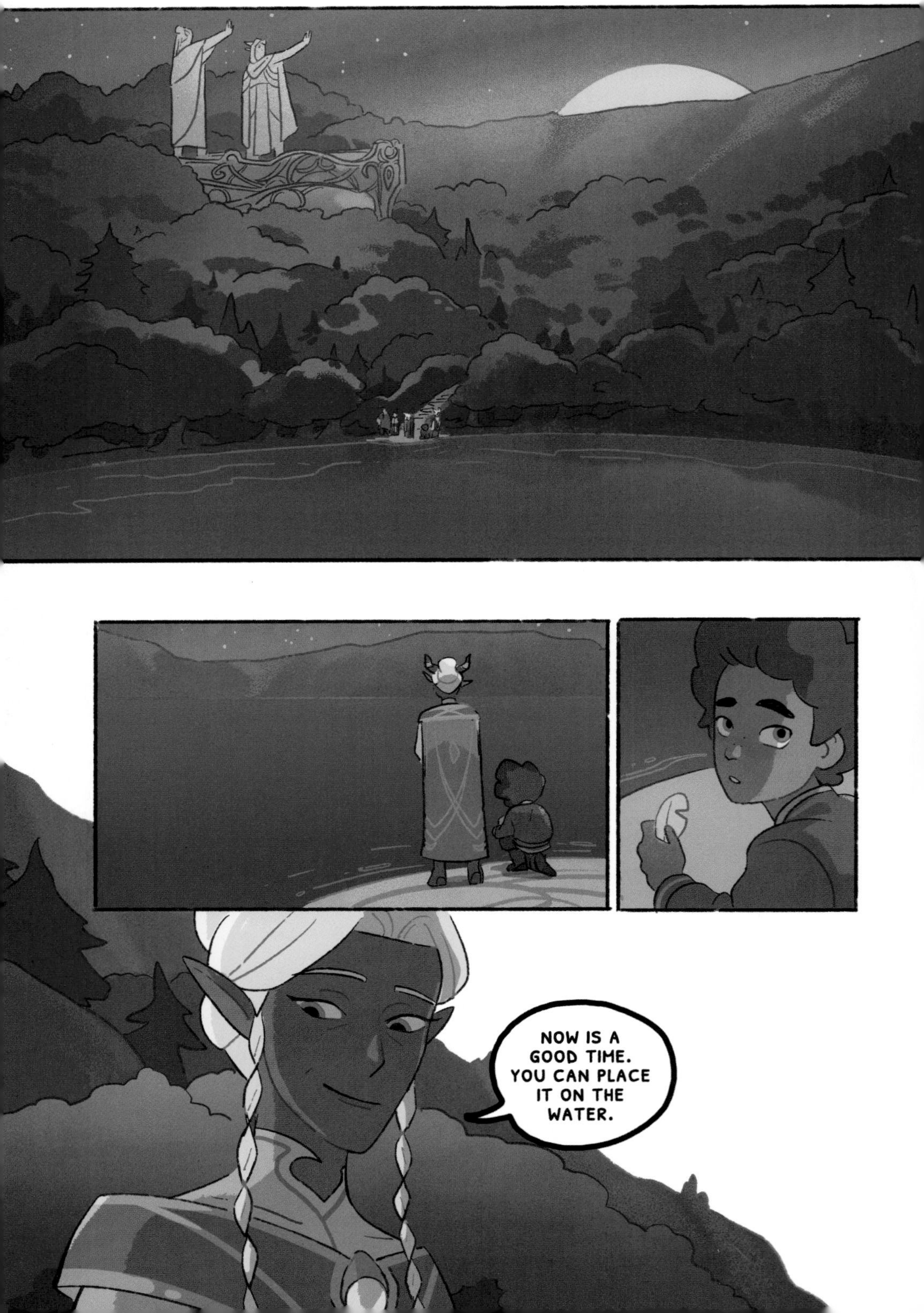
NOW IS A GOOD TIME. YOU CAN PLACE IT ON THE WATER.

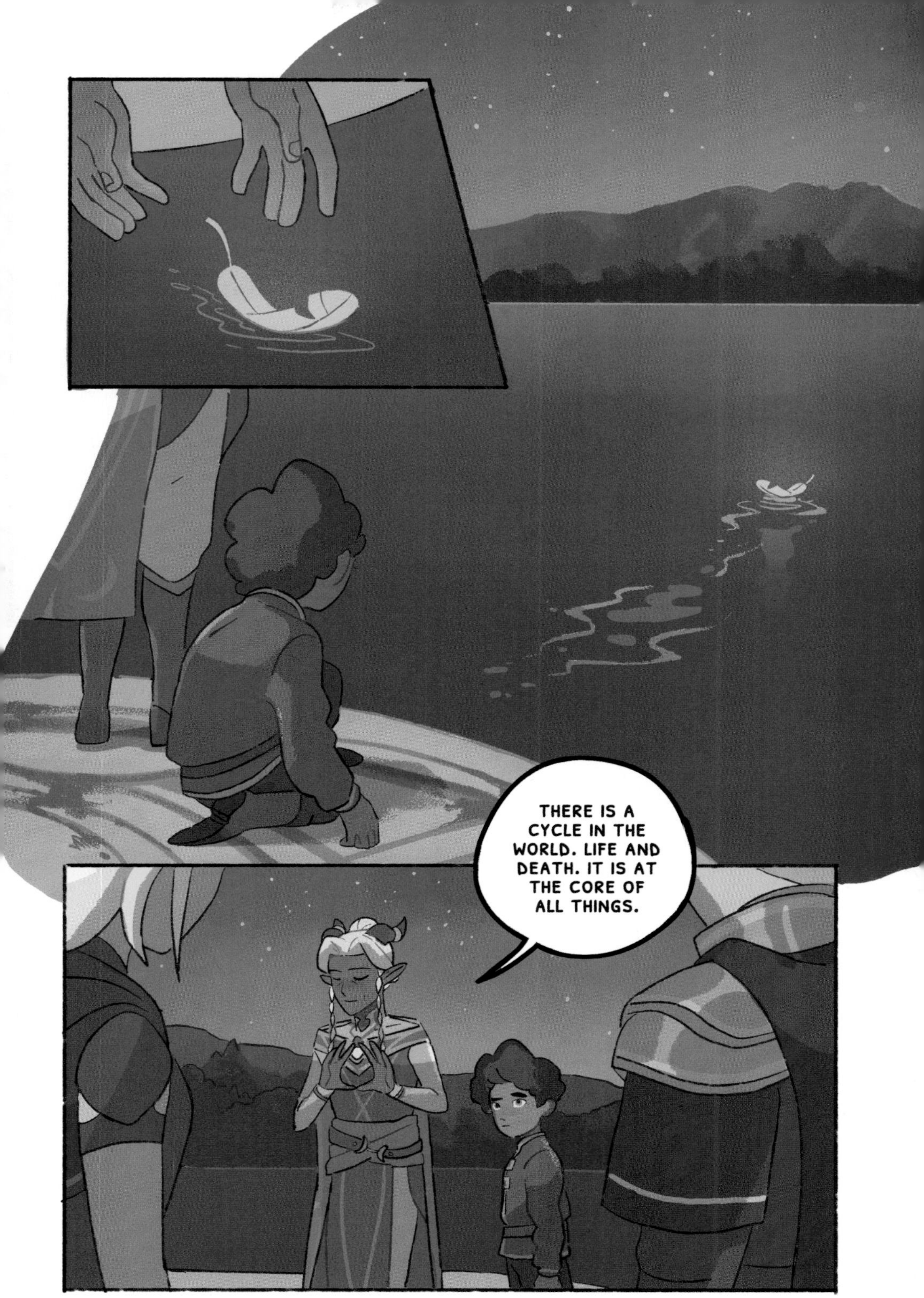
THERE IS A CYCLE IN THE WORLD. LIFE AND DEATH. IT IS AT THE CORE OF ALL THINGS.

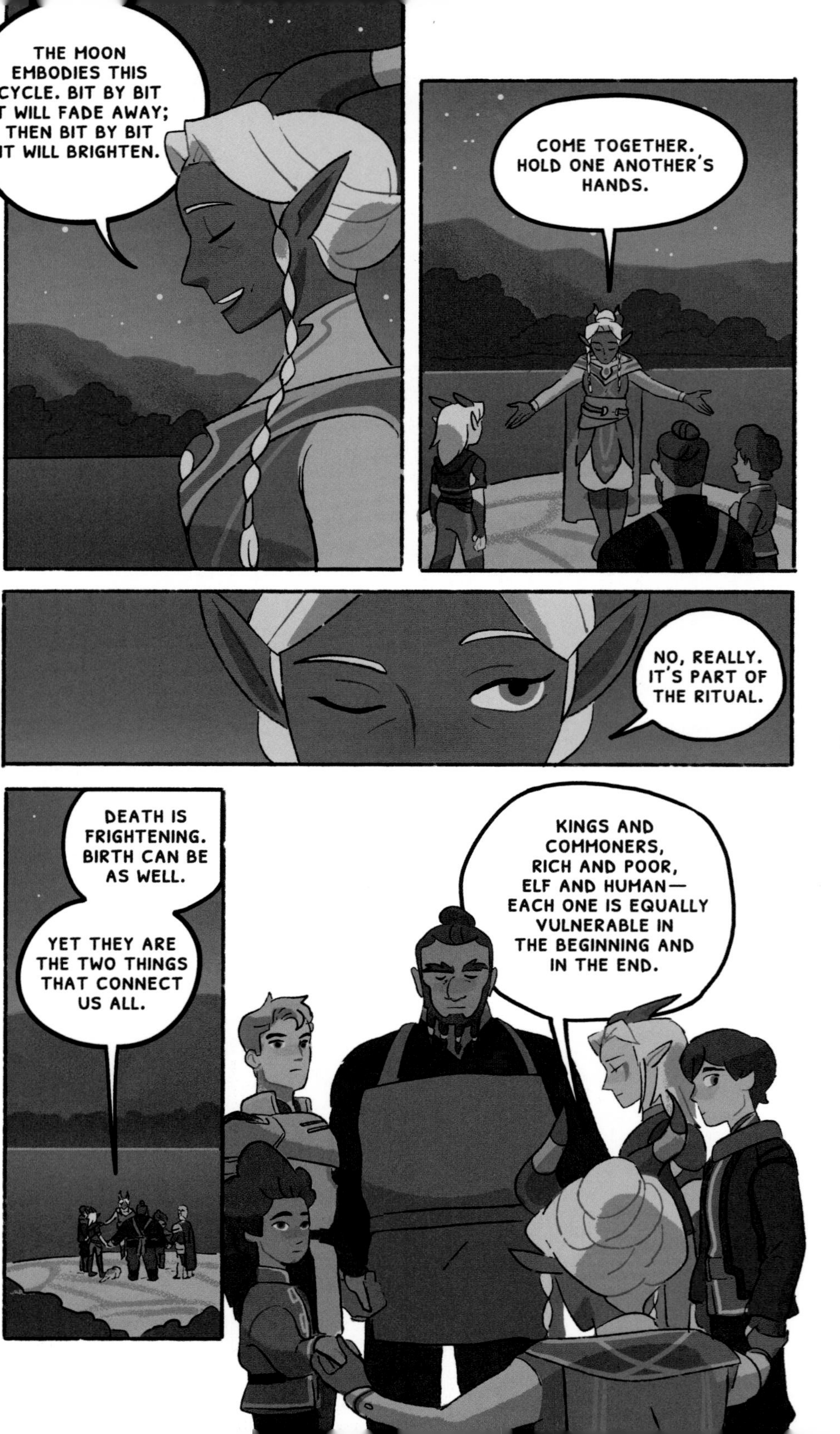
THE MOON EMBODIES THIS CYCLE. BIT BY BIT IT WILL FADE AWAY; THEN BIT BY BIT IT WILL BRIGHTEN.
COME TOGETHER. HOLD ONE ANOTHER'S HANDS.
NO, REALLY. IT'S PART OF THE RITUAL.
DEATH IS FRIGHTENING. BIRTH CAN BE AS WELL.
YET THEY ARE THE TWO THINGS THAT CONNECT US ALL.
KINGS AND COMMONERS, RICH AND POOR, ELF AND HUMAN— EACH ONE IS EQUALLY VULNERABLE IN THE BEGINNING AND IN THE END.

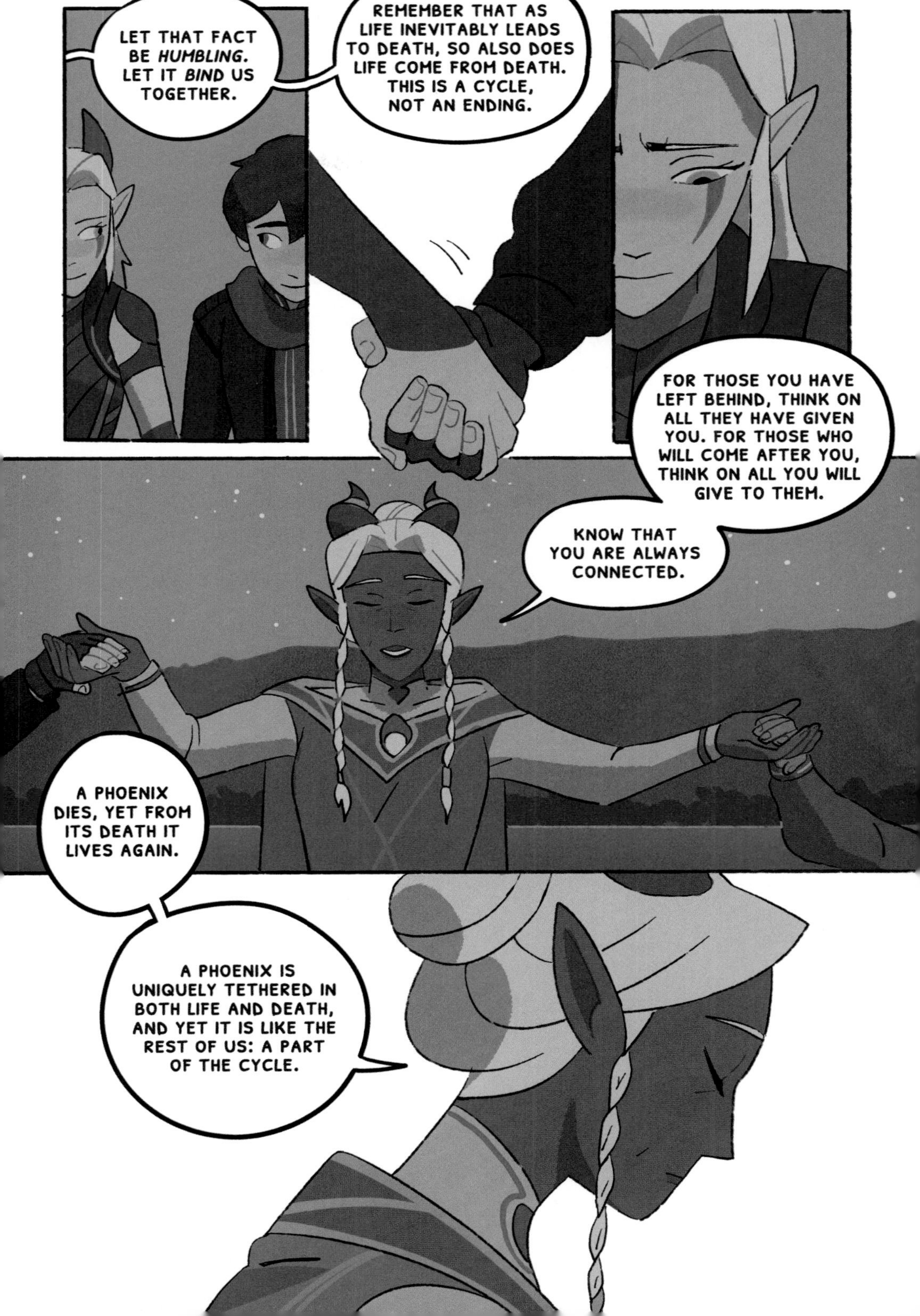
LET THAT FACT BE *HUMBLING*. LET IT *BIND* US TOGETHER.
REMEMBER THAT AS LIFE INEVITABLY LEADS TO DEATH, SO ALSO DOES LIFE COME FROM DEATH. THIS IS A CYCLE, NOT AN ENDING.
FOR THOSE YOU HAVE LEFT BEHIND, THINK ON ALL THEY HAVE GIVEN YOU. FOR THOSE WHO WILL COME AFTER YOU, THINK ON ALL YOU WILL GIVE TO THEM.
KNOW THAT YOU ARE ALWAYS CONNECTED.
A PHOENIX DIES, YET FROM ITS DEATH IT LIVES AGAIN.
A PHOENIX IS UNIQUELY TETHERED IN BOTH LIFE AND DEATH, AND YET IT IS LIKE THE REST OF US: A PART OF THE CYCLE.

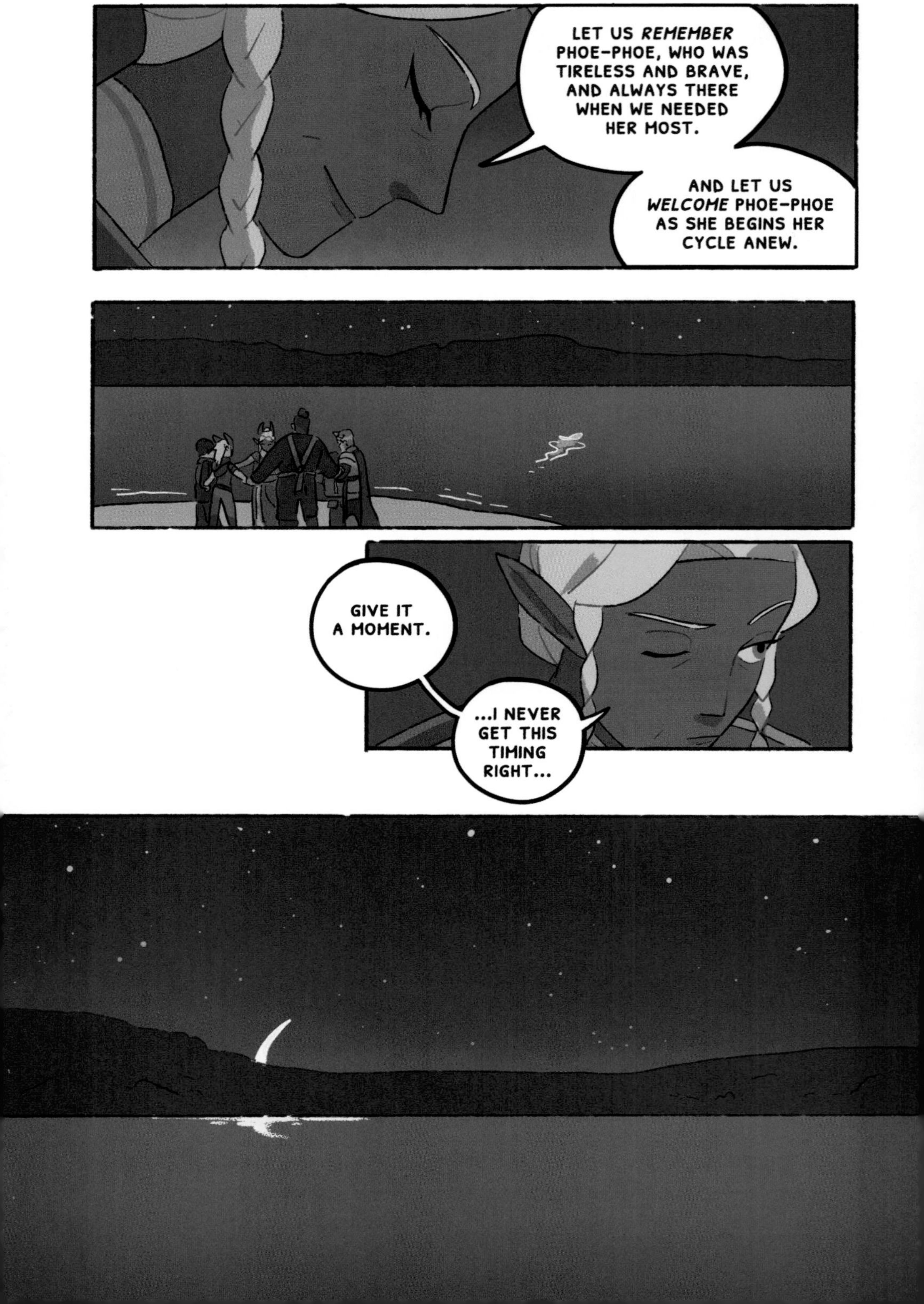
LET US *REMEMBER* PHOE-PHOE, WHO WAS TIRELESS AND BRAVE, AND ALWAYS THERE WHEN WE NEEDED HER MOST.
AND LET US *WELCOME* PHOE-PHOE AS SHE BEGINS HER CYCLE ANEW.
GIVE IT A MOMENT.
...I NEVER GET THIS TIMING RIGHT...

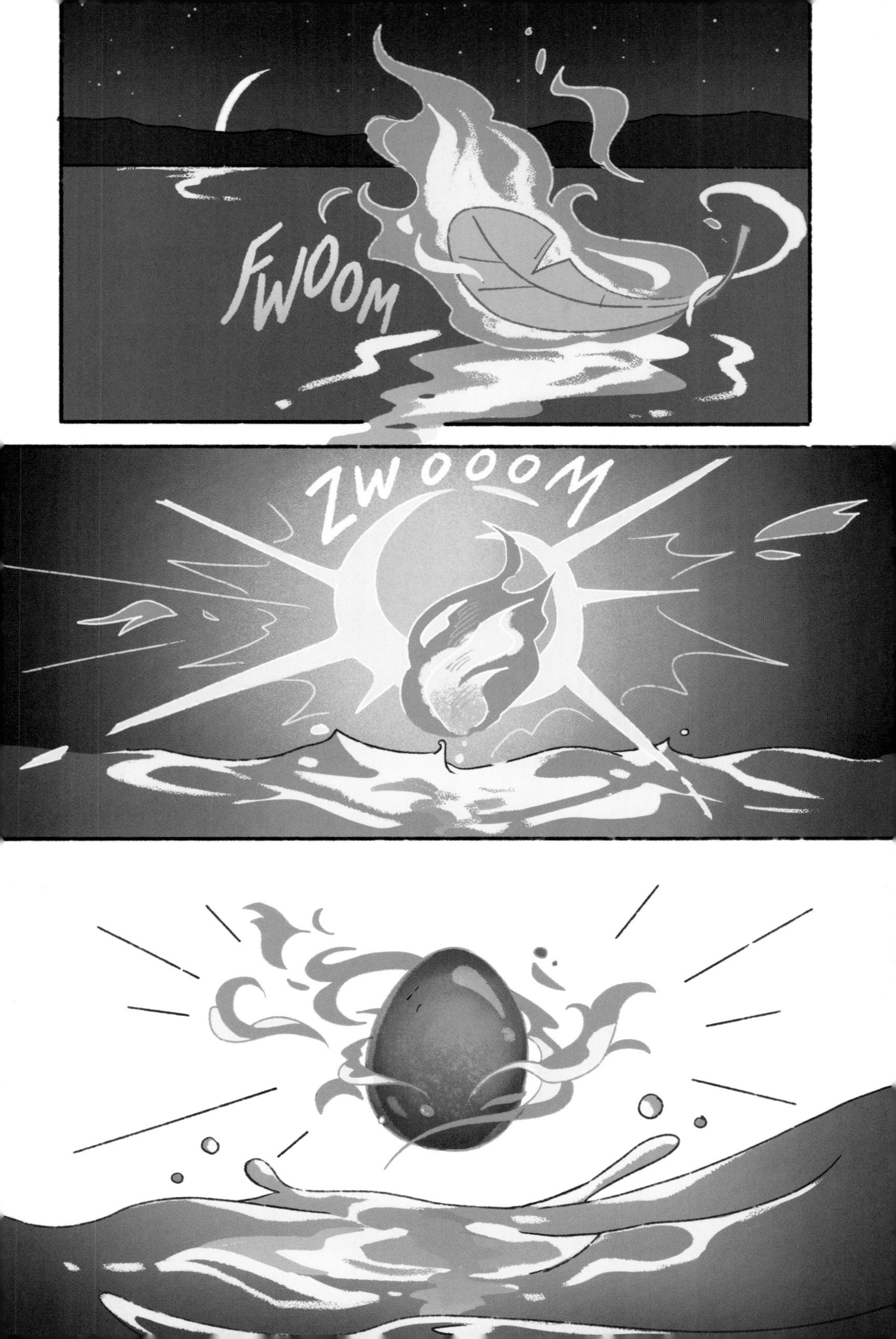
FWOOM
ZWOOOM

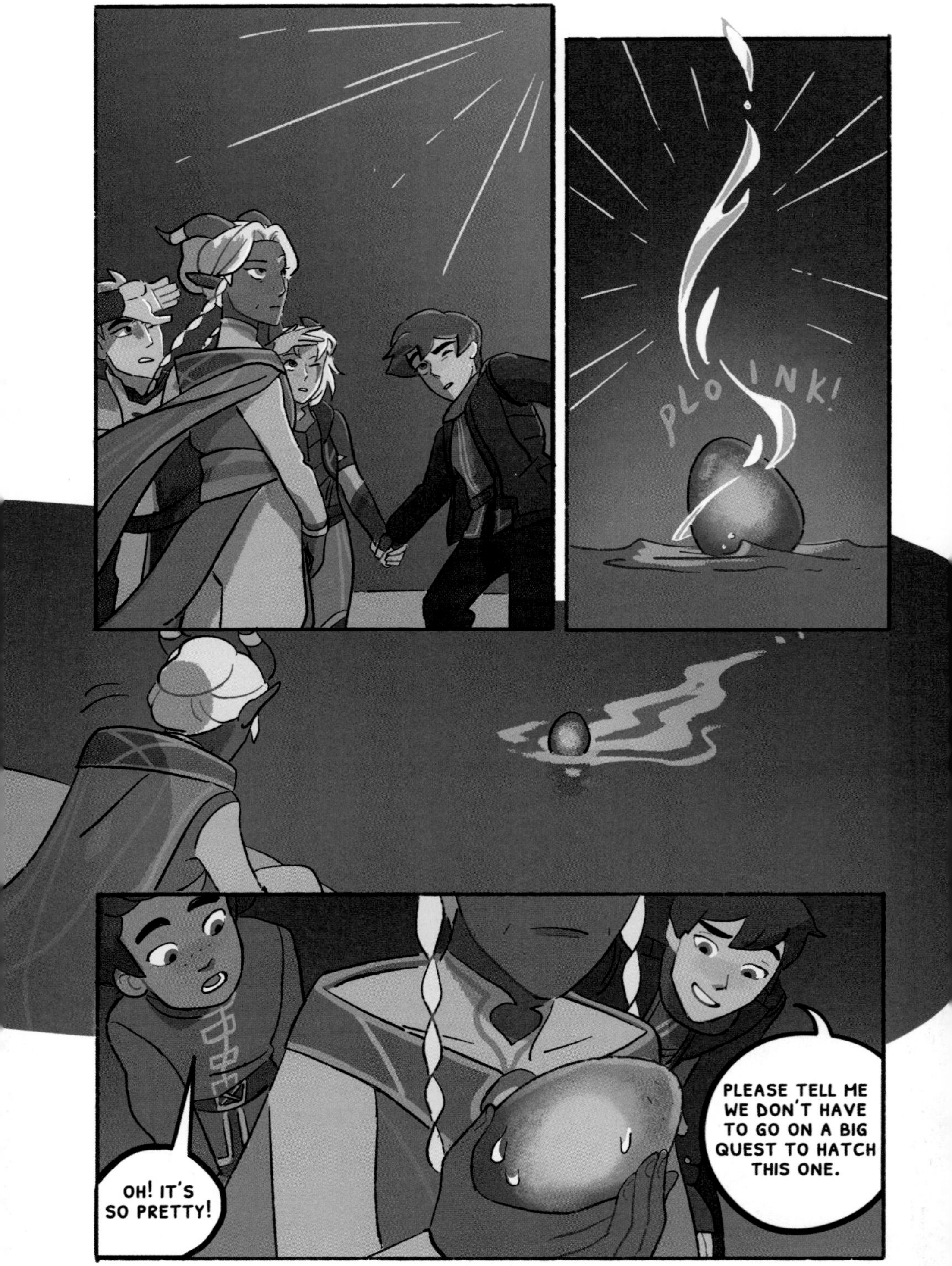
PLOINK!
OH! IT'S SO PRETTY!
PLEASE TELL ME WE DON'T HAVE TO GO ON A BIG QUEST TO HATCH THIS ONE.

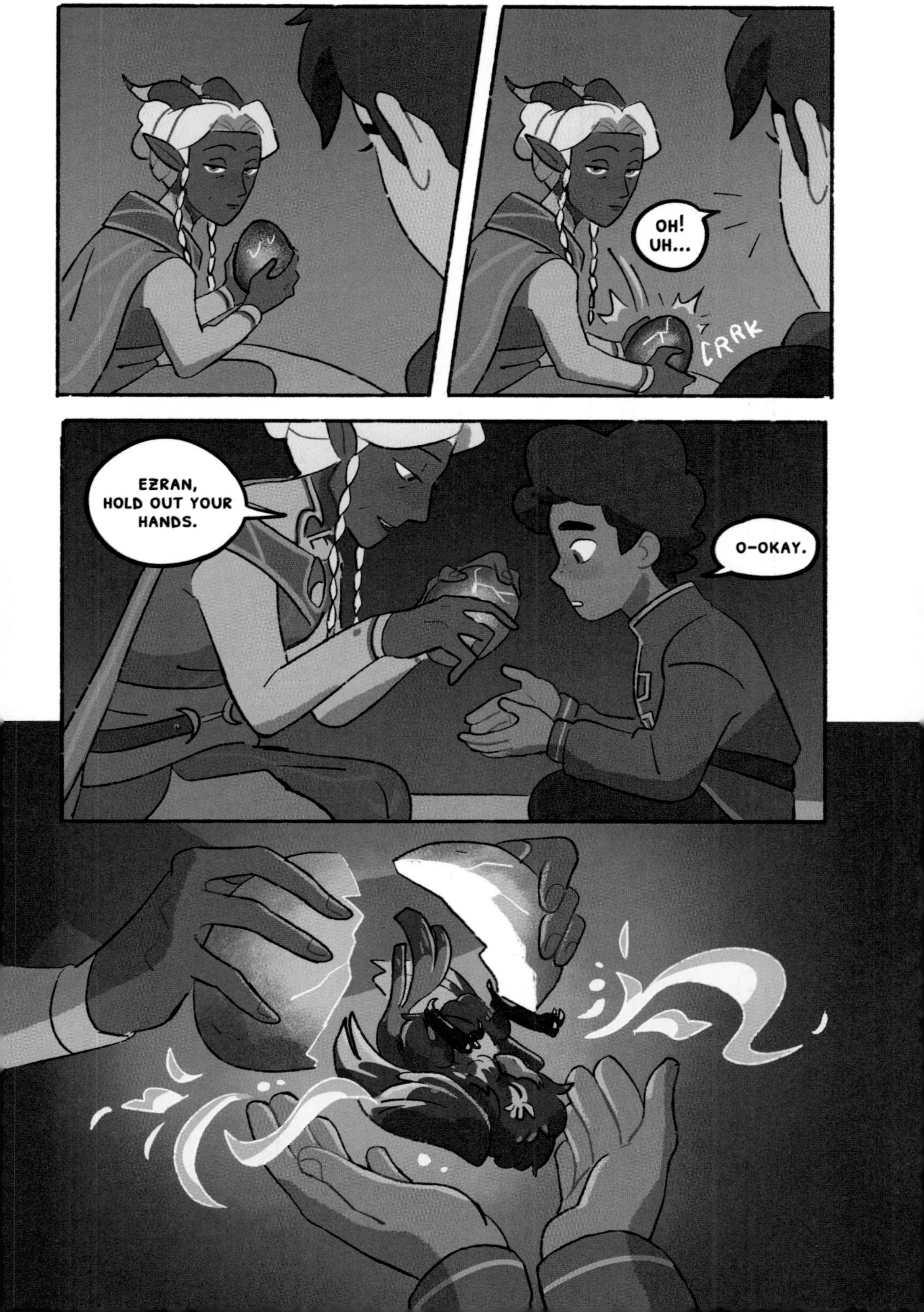
OH!
UH...
CRRK
EZRAN, HOLD OUT YOUR HANDS.
O-OKAY.

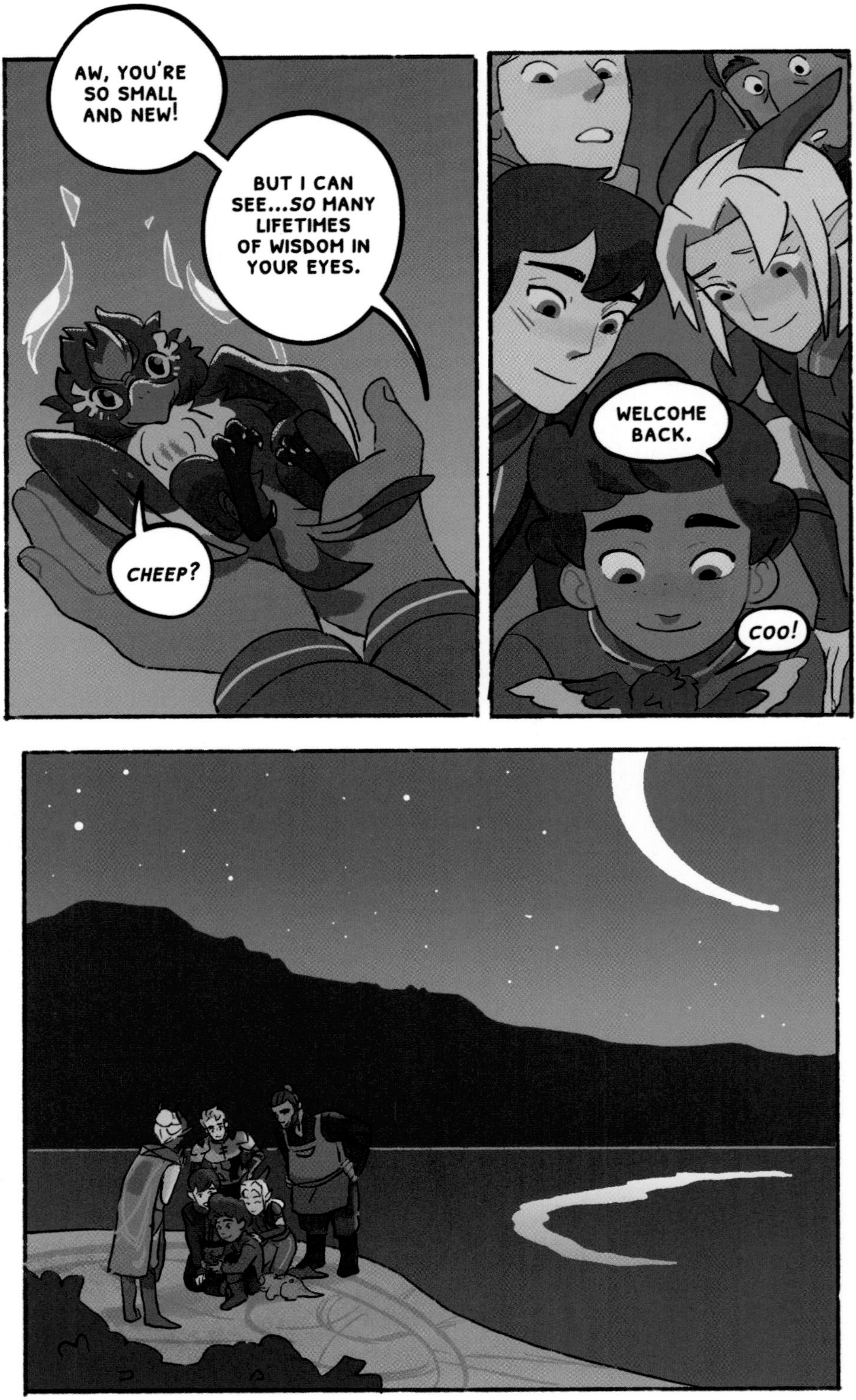
AW, YOU'RE SO SMALL AND NEW!
BUT I CAN SEE...SO MANY LIFETIMES OF WISDOM IN YOUR EYES.
CHEEP?
WELCOME BACK.
COO!

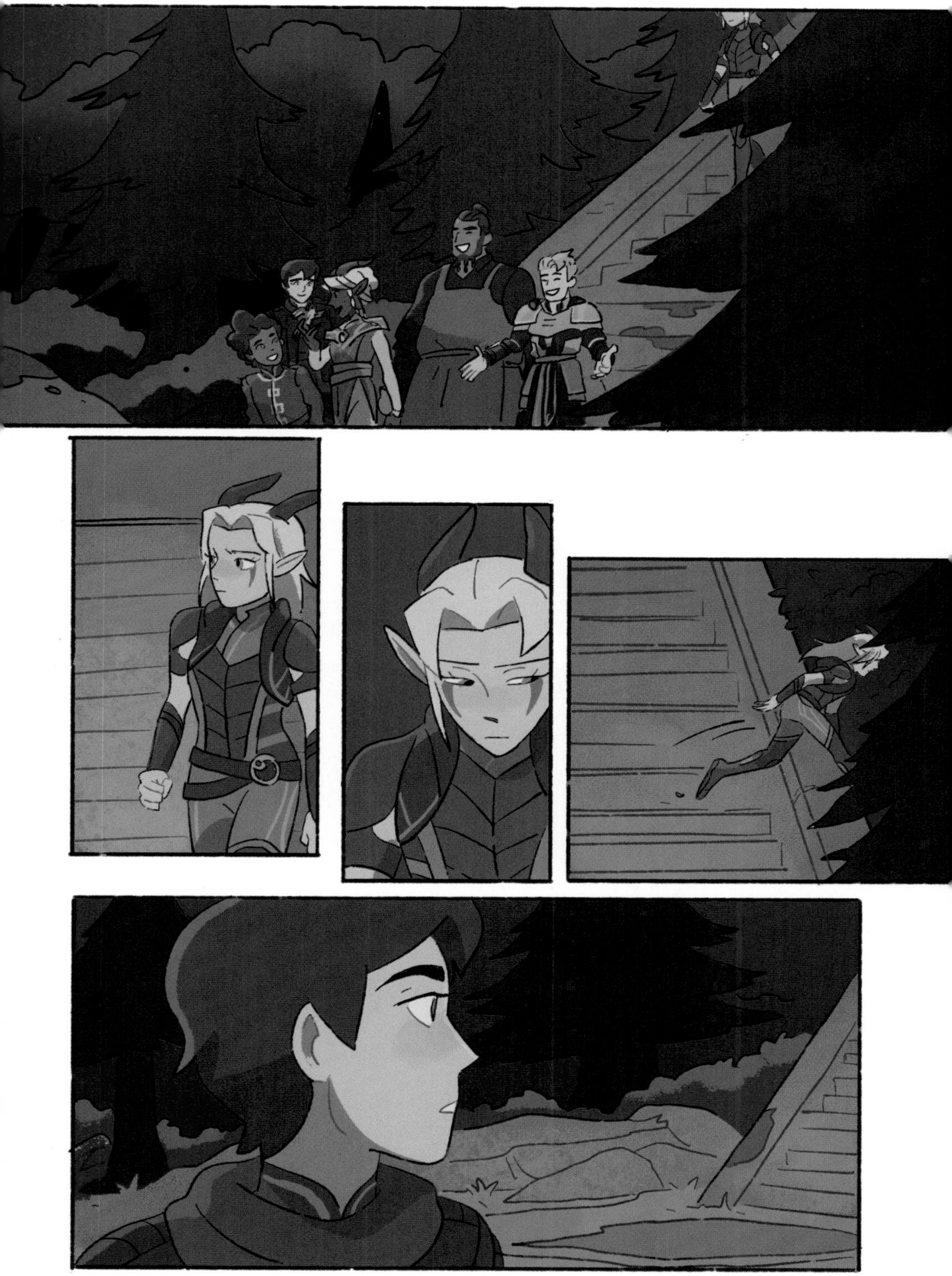

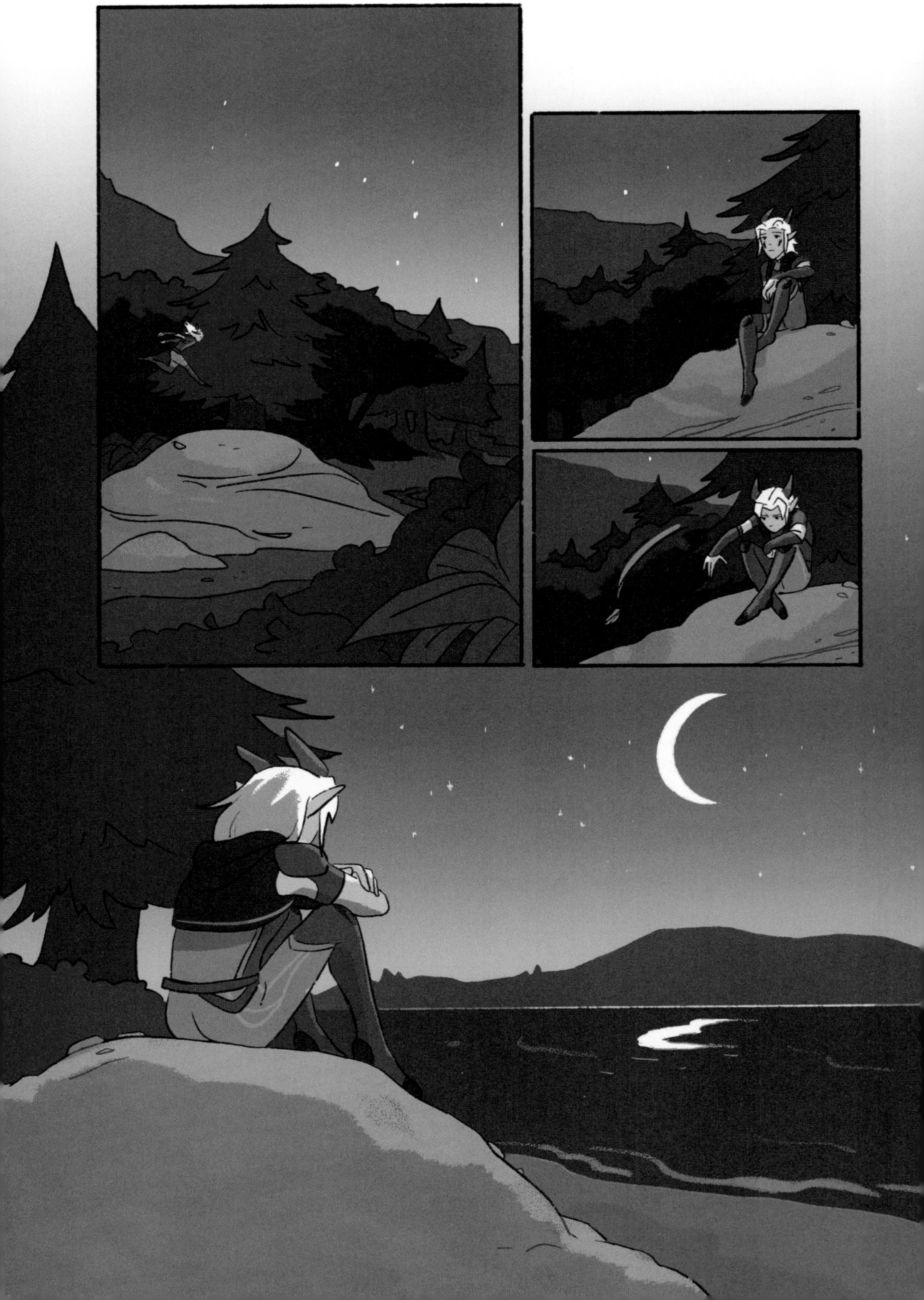

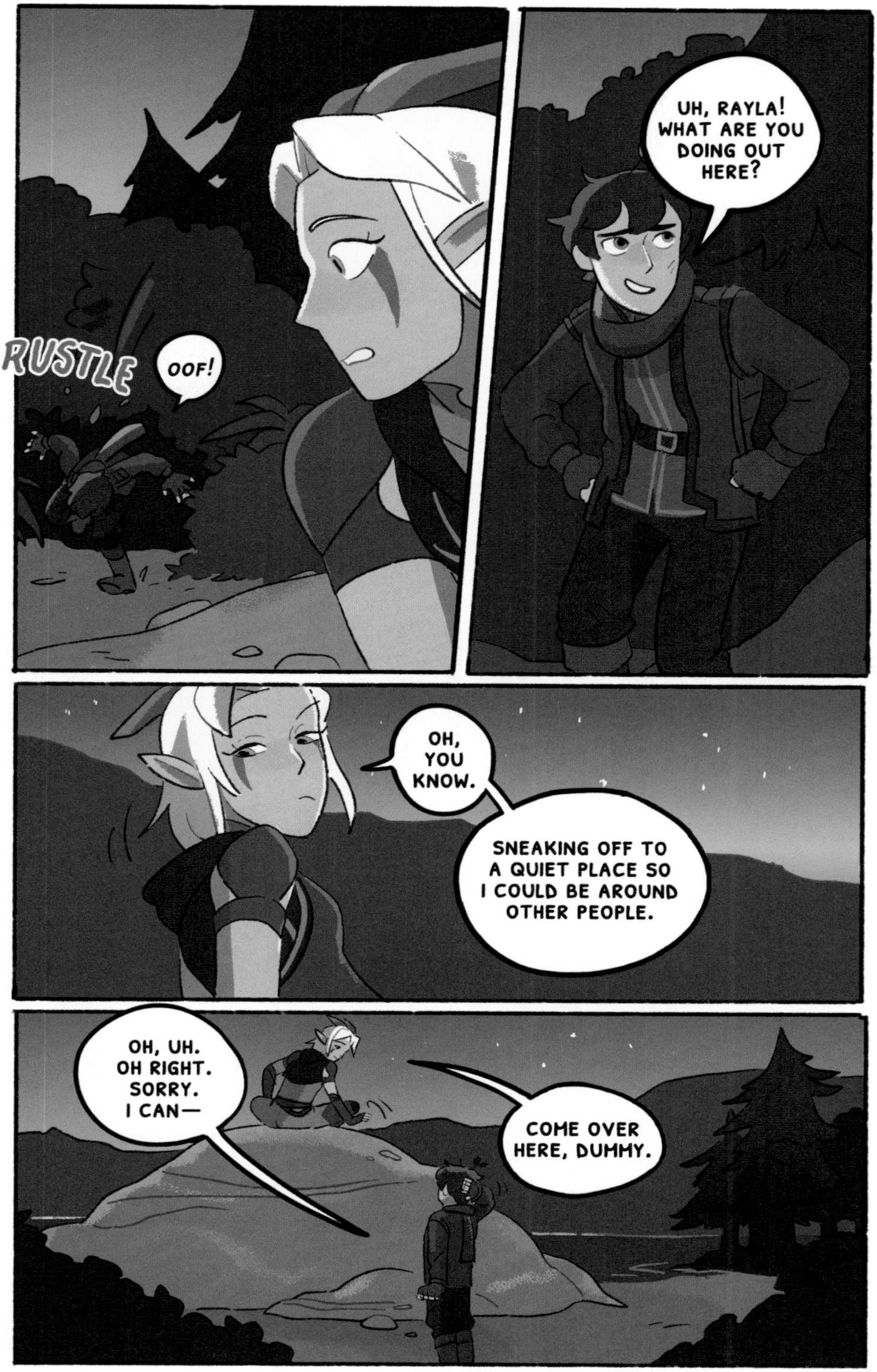
RUSTLE
OOF!
UH, RAYLA! WHAT ARE YOU DOING OUT HERE?
OH, YOU KNOW.
SNEAKING OFF TO A QUIET PLACE SO I COULD BE AROUND OTHER PEOPLE.
OH, UH. OH RIGHT. SORRY. I CAN—
COME OVER HERE, DUMMY.

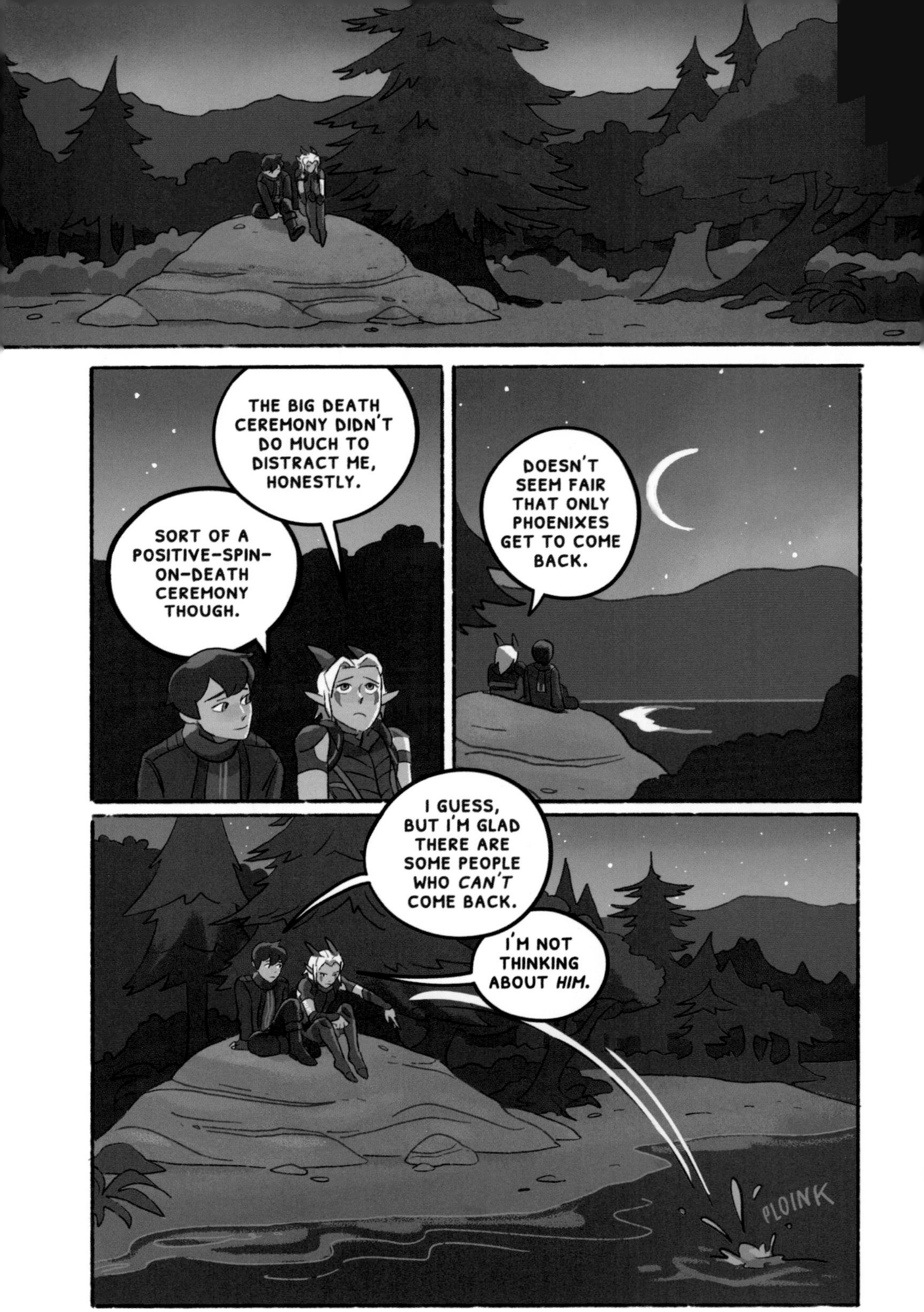
SORT OF A POSITIVE-SPIN-ON-DEATH CEREMONY THOUGH.
THE BIG DEATH CEREMONY DIDN'T DO MUCH TO DISTRACT ME, HONESTLY.
DOESN'T SEEM FAIR THAT ONLY PHOENIXES GET TO COME BACK.
I GUESS, BUT I'M GLAD THERE ARE SOME PEOPLE WHO *CAN'T* COME BACK.
I'M NOT THINKING ABOUT *HIM*.
PLOINK

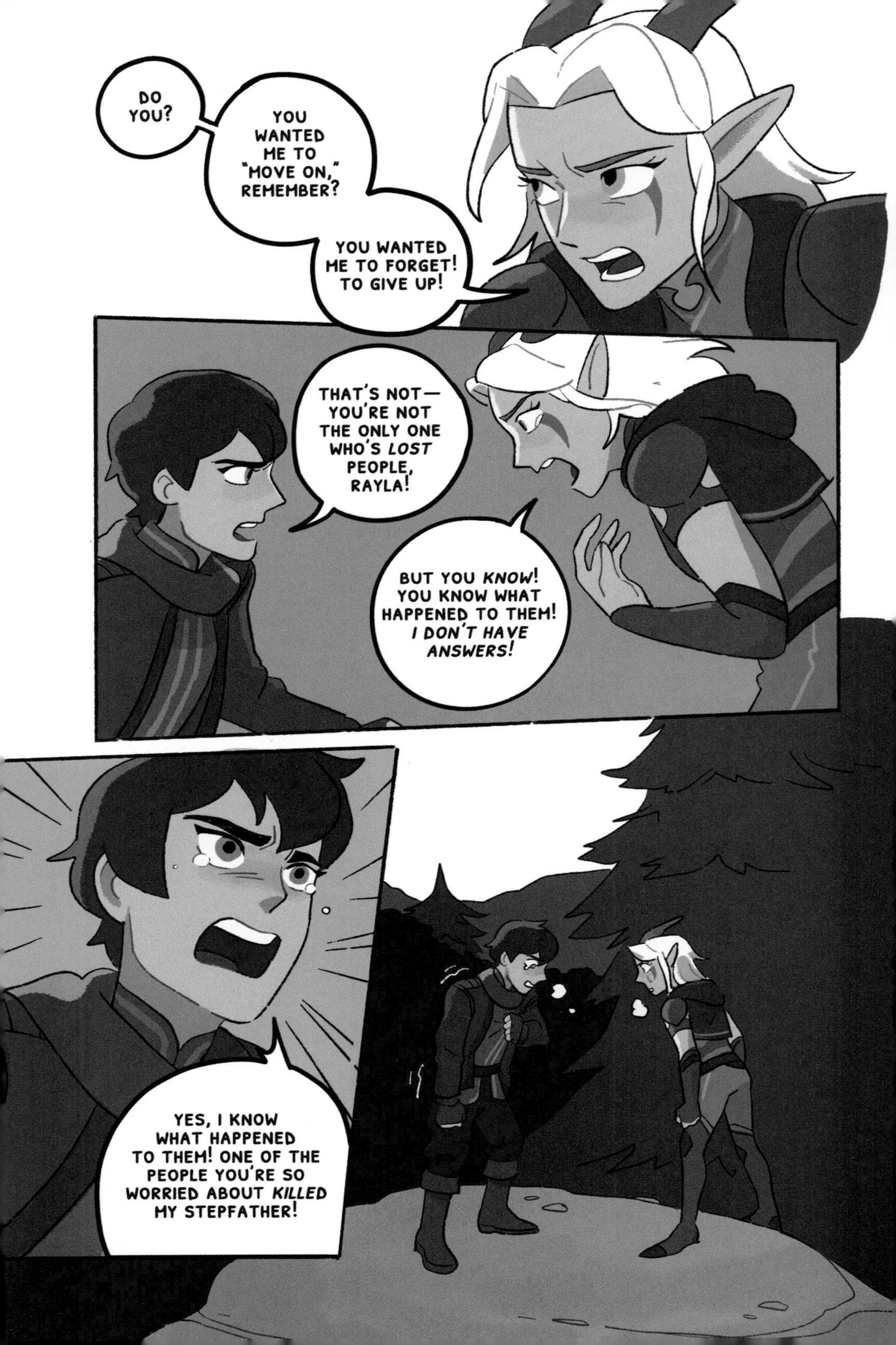
DO YOU?
YOU WANTED ME TO "MOVE ON," REMEMBER?
YOU WANTED ME TO FORGET! TO GIVE UP!
THAT'S NOT— YOU'RE NOT THE ONLY ONE WHO'S *LOST* PEOPLE, RAYLA!
BUT YOU *KNOW*! YOU KNOW WHAT HAPPENED TO THEM! *I DON'T HAVE ANSWERS*!
YES, I KNOW WHAT HAPPENED TO THEM! ONE OF THE PEOPLE YOU'RE SO WORRIED ABOUT *KILLED* MY STEPFATHER!

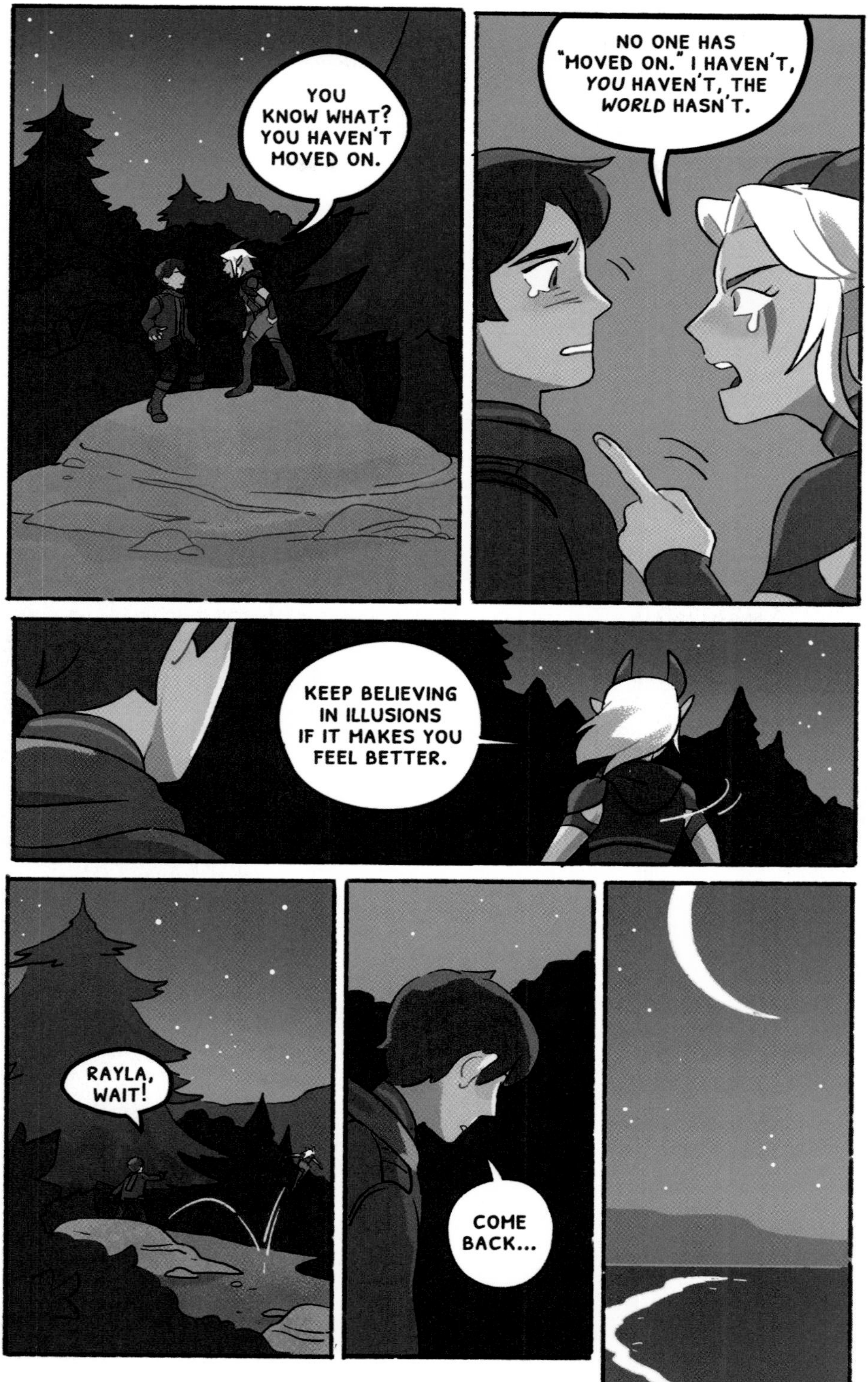
YOU KNOW WHAT? YOU HAVEN'T MOVED ON.
NO ONE HAS "MOVED ON." I HAVEN'T, *YOU* HAVEN'T, THE *WORLD* HASN'T.
KEEP BELIEVING IN ILLUSIONS IF IT MAKES YOU FEEL BETTER.
RAYLA, WAIT!
COME BACK...

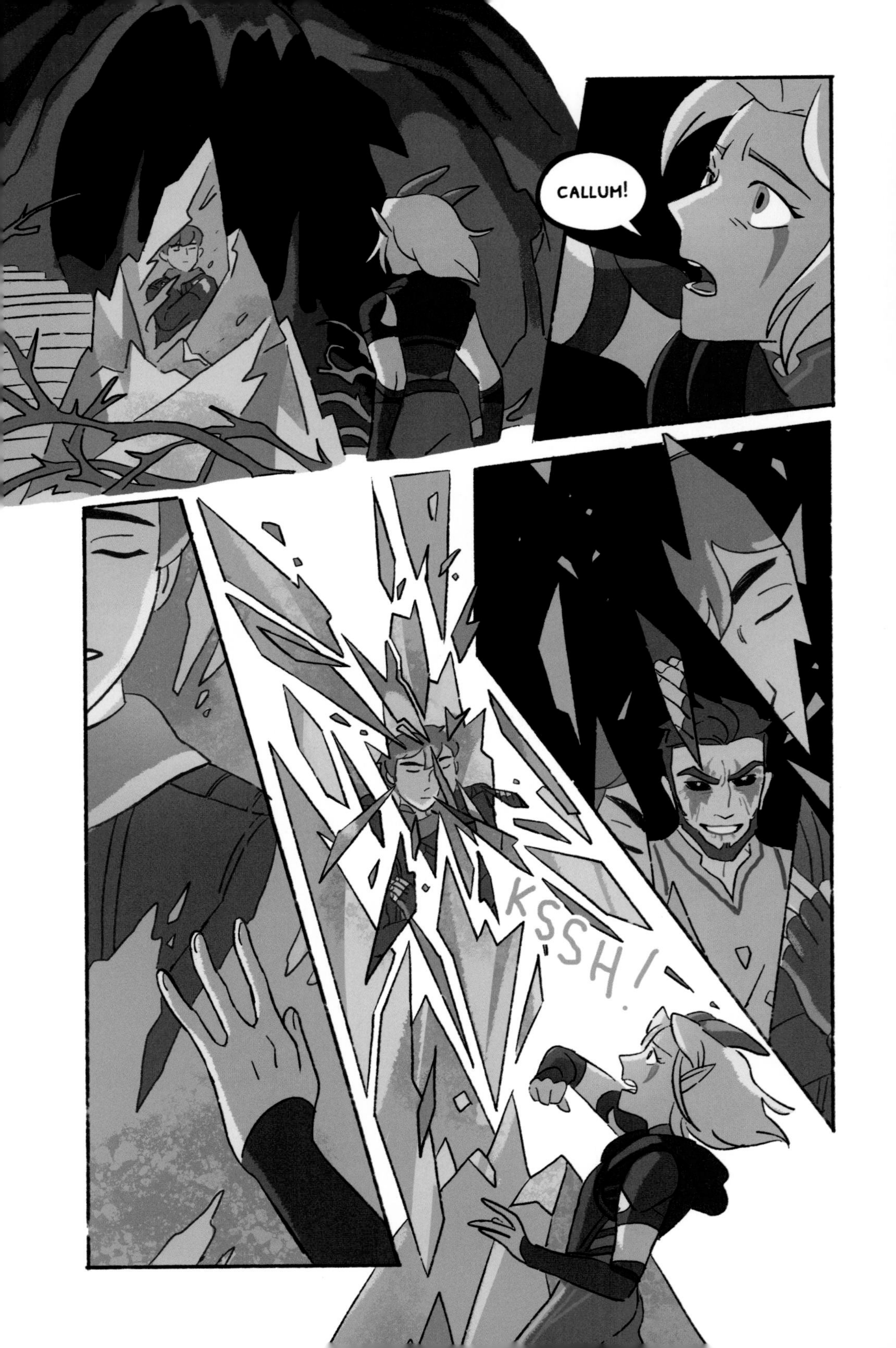
CALLUM!
KSSH!

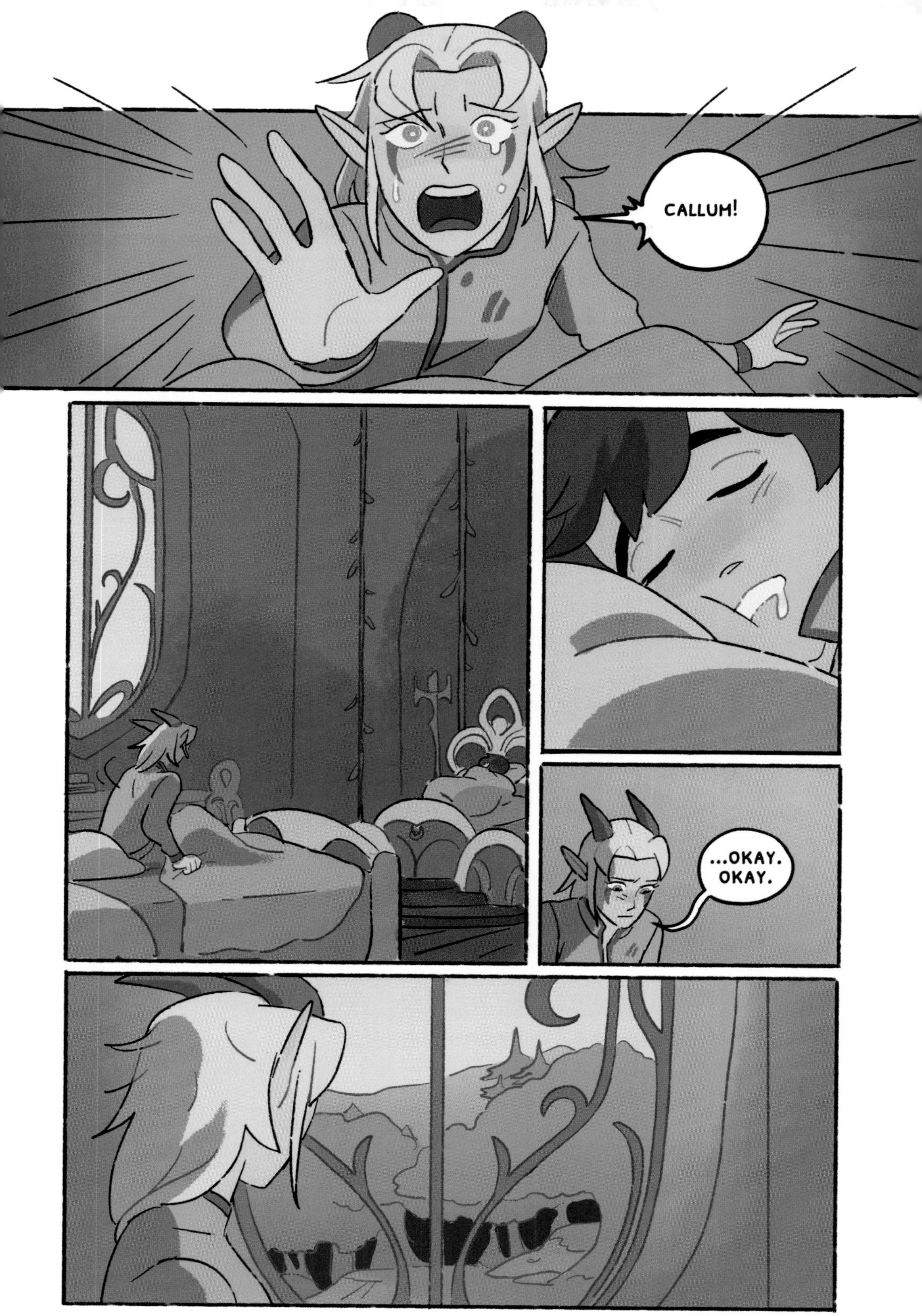
CALLUM!
...OKAY.
OKAY.

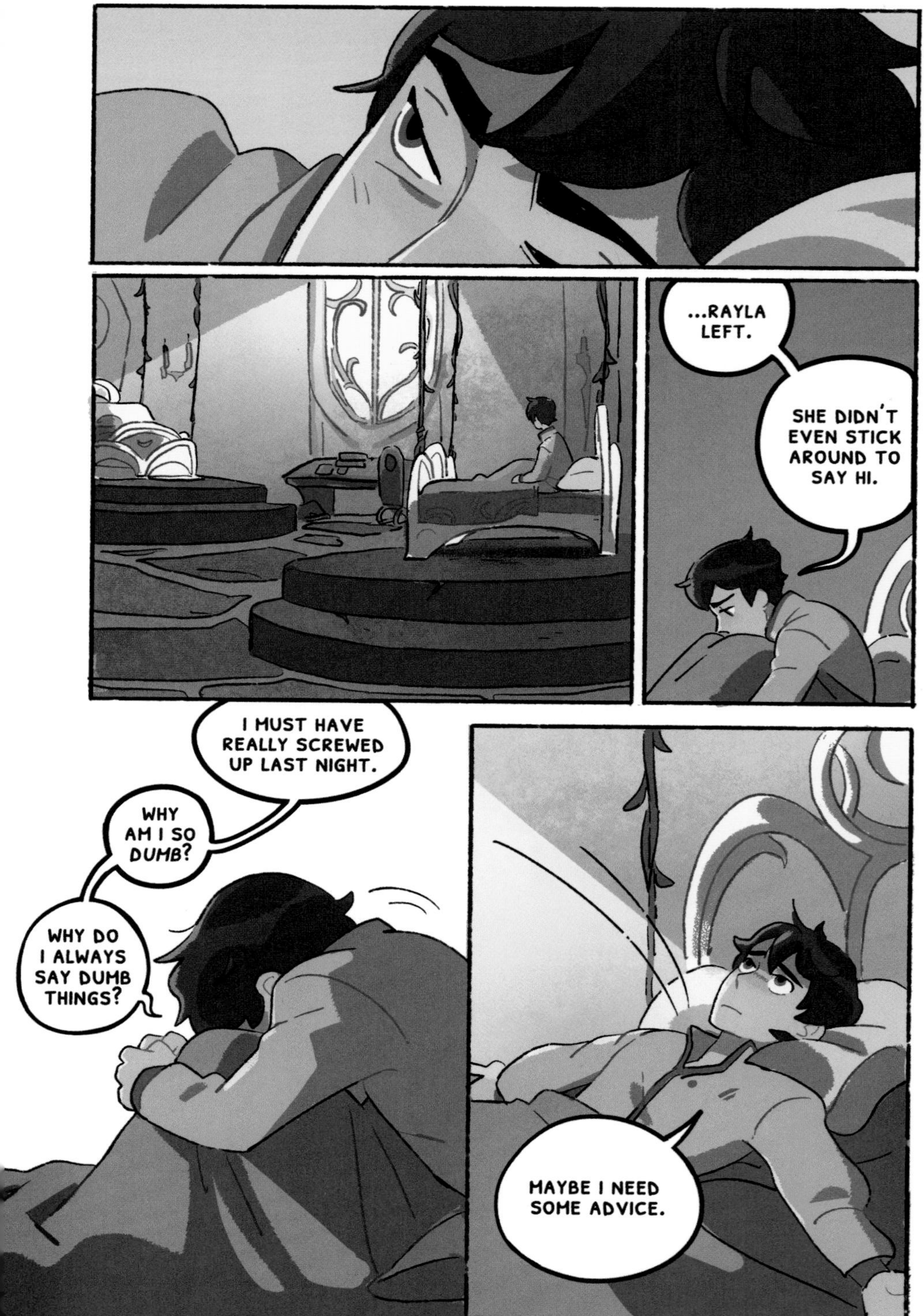
...RAYLA LEFT.
SHE DIDN'T EVEN STICK AROUND TO SAY HI.
I MUST HAVE REALLY SCREWED UP LAST NIGHT.
WHY AM I SO DUMB?
WHY DO I ALWAYS SAY DUMB THINGS?
MAYBE I NEED SOME ADVICE.

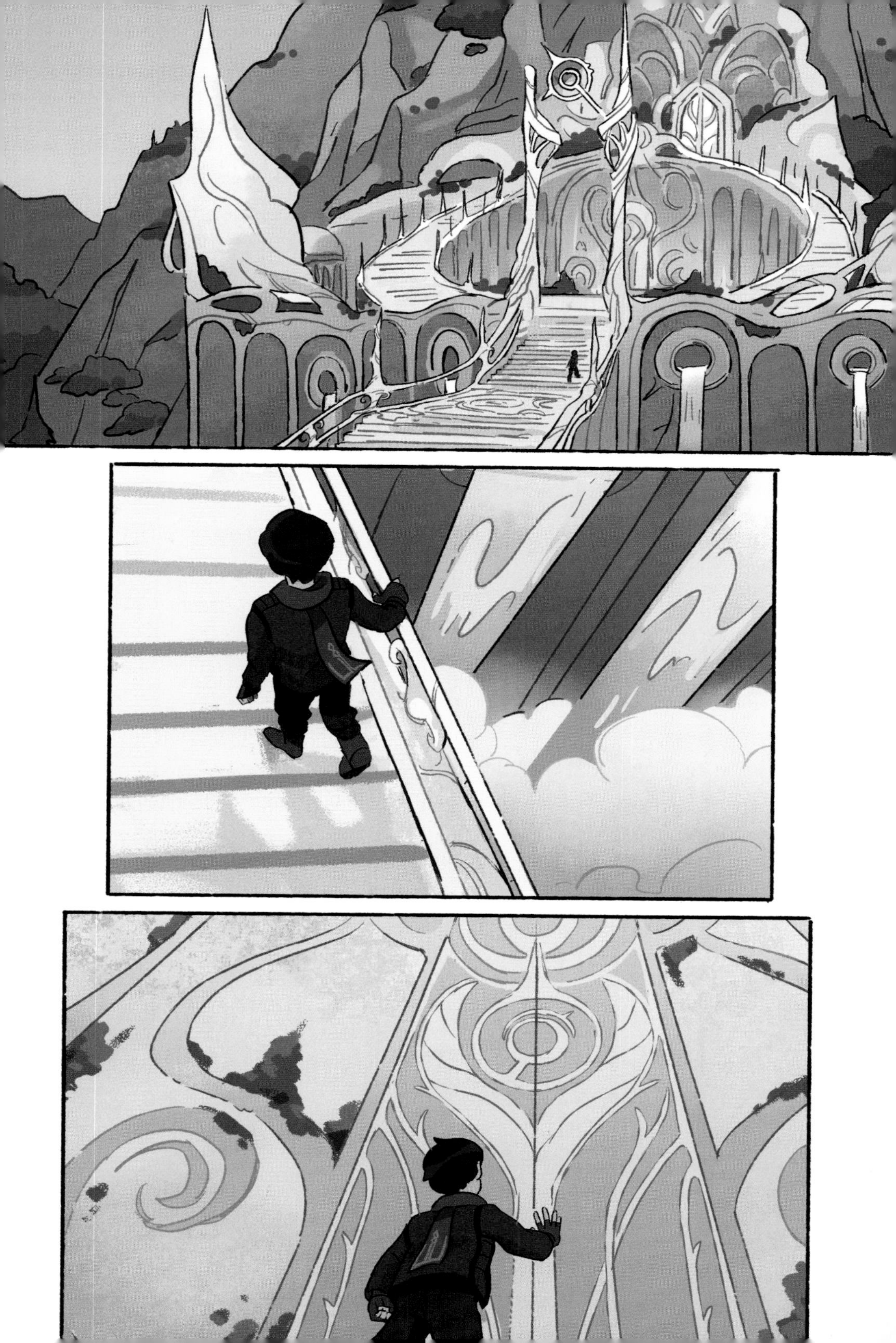

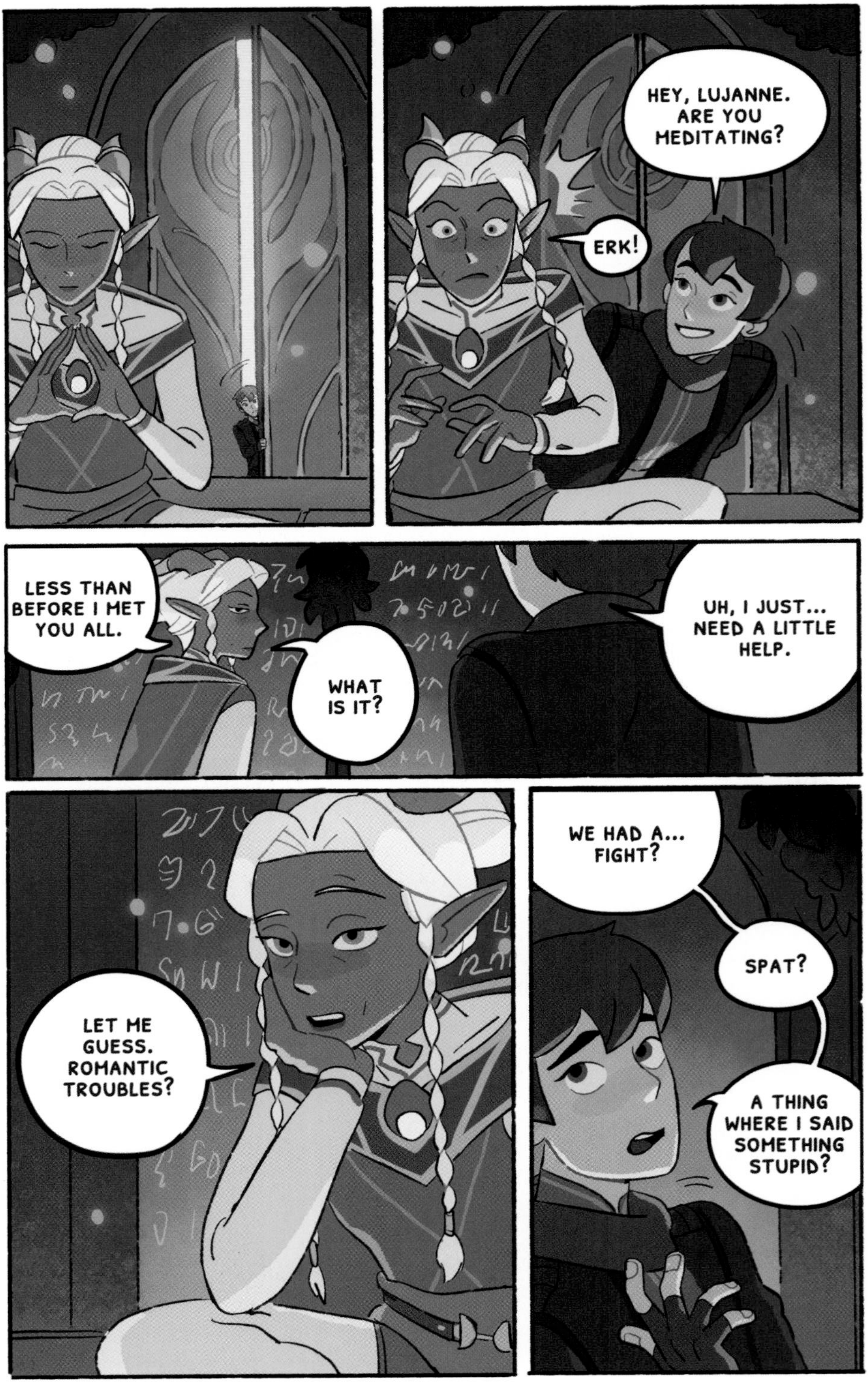
HEY, LUJANNE. ARE YOU MEDITATING?
ERK!
UH, I JUST... NEED A LITTLE HELP.
WHAT IS IT?
LESS THAN BEFORE I MET YOU ALL.
LET ME GUESS. ROMANTIC TROUBLES?
WE HAD A... FIGHT?
SPAT?
A THING WHERE I SAID SOMETHING STUPID?

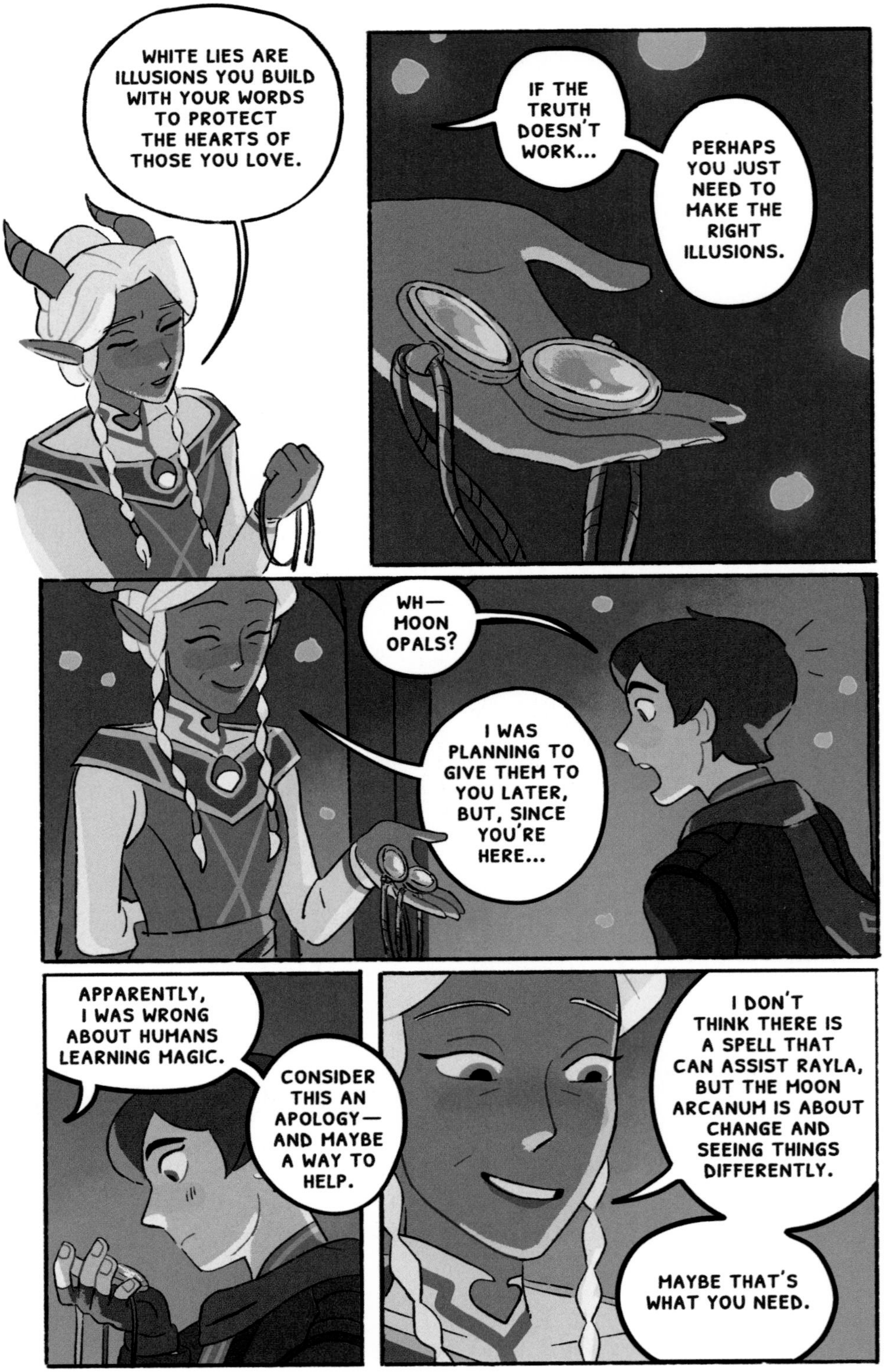
WHITE LIES ARE ILLUSIONS YOU BUILD WITH YOUR WORDS TO PROTECT THE HEARTS OF THOSE YOU LOVE.
IF THE TRUTH DOESN'T WORK...
PERHAPS YOU JUST NEED TO MAKE THE RIGHT ILLUSIONS.
WH— MOON OPALS?
I WAS PLANNING TO GIVE THEM TO YOU LATER, BUT, SINCE YOU'RE HERE...
APPARENTLY, I WAS WRONG ABOUT HUMANS LEARNING MAGIC.
CONSIDER THIS AN APOLOGY— AND MAYBE A WAY TO HELP.
I DON'T THINK THERE IS A SPELL THAT CAN ASSIST RAYLA, BUT THE MOON ARCANUM IS ABOUT CHANGE AND SEEING THINGS DIFFERENTLY.
MAYBE THAT'S WHAT YOU NEED.

47

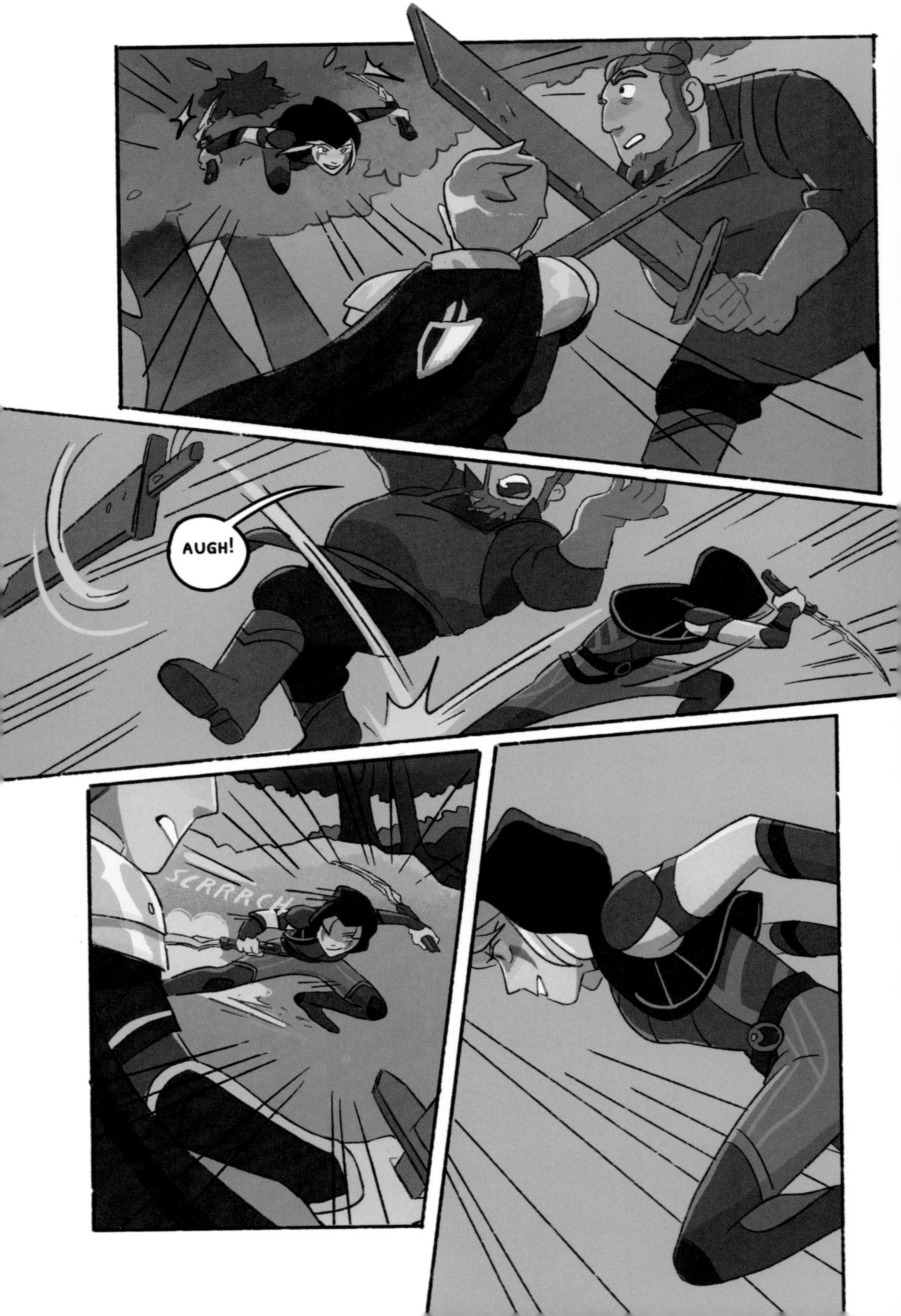
AUGH!
SCRRRCH

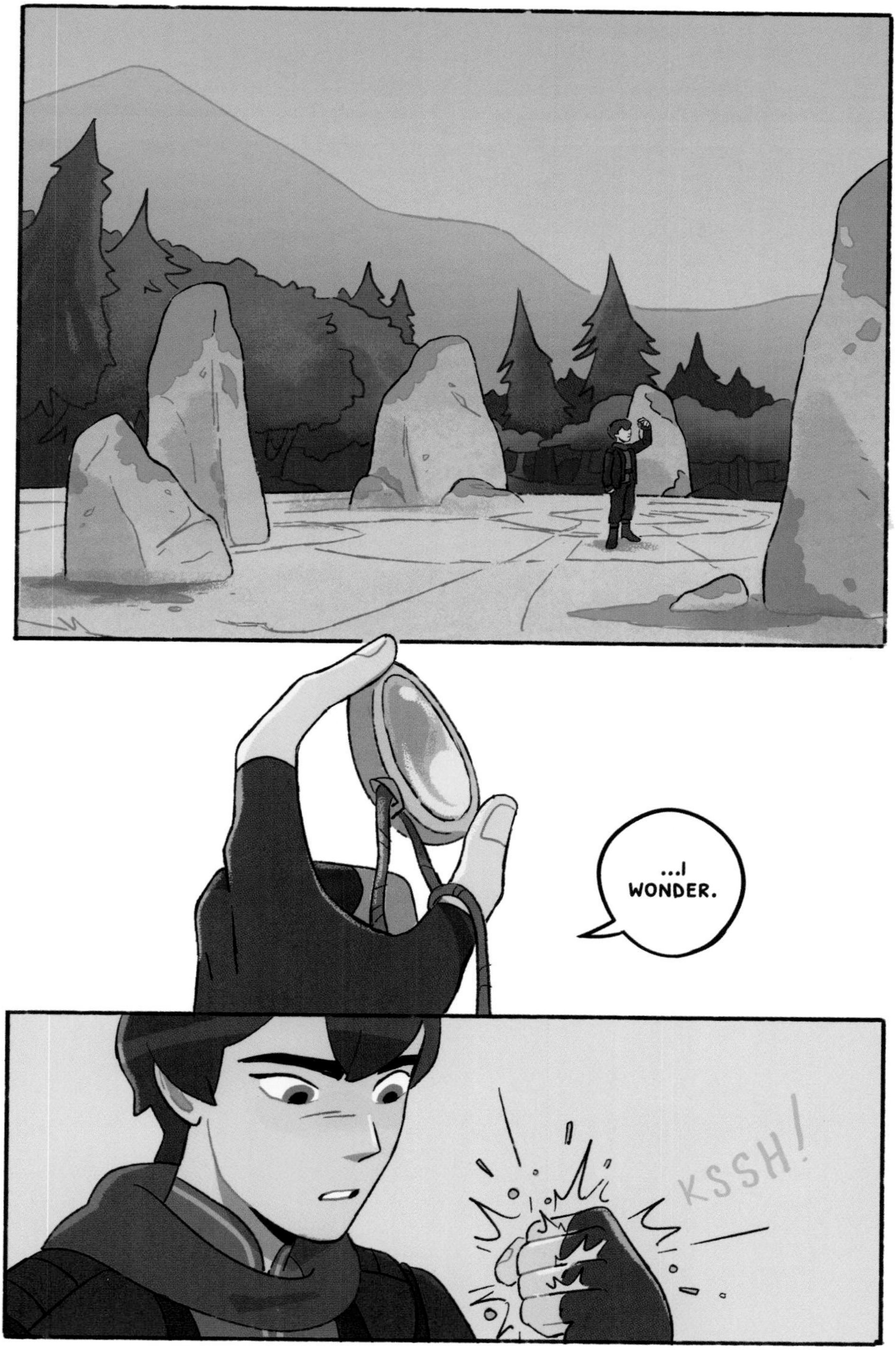
...I WONDER.
KSSH!

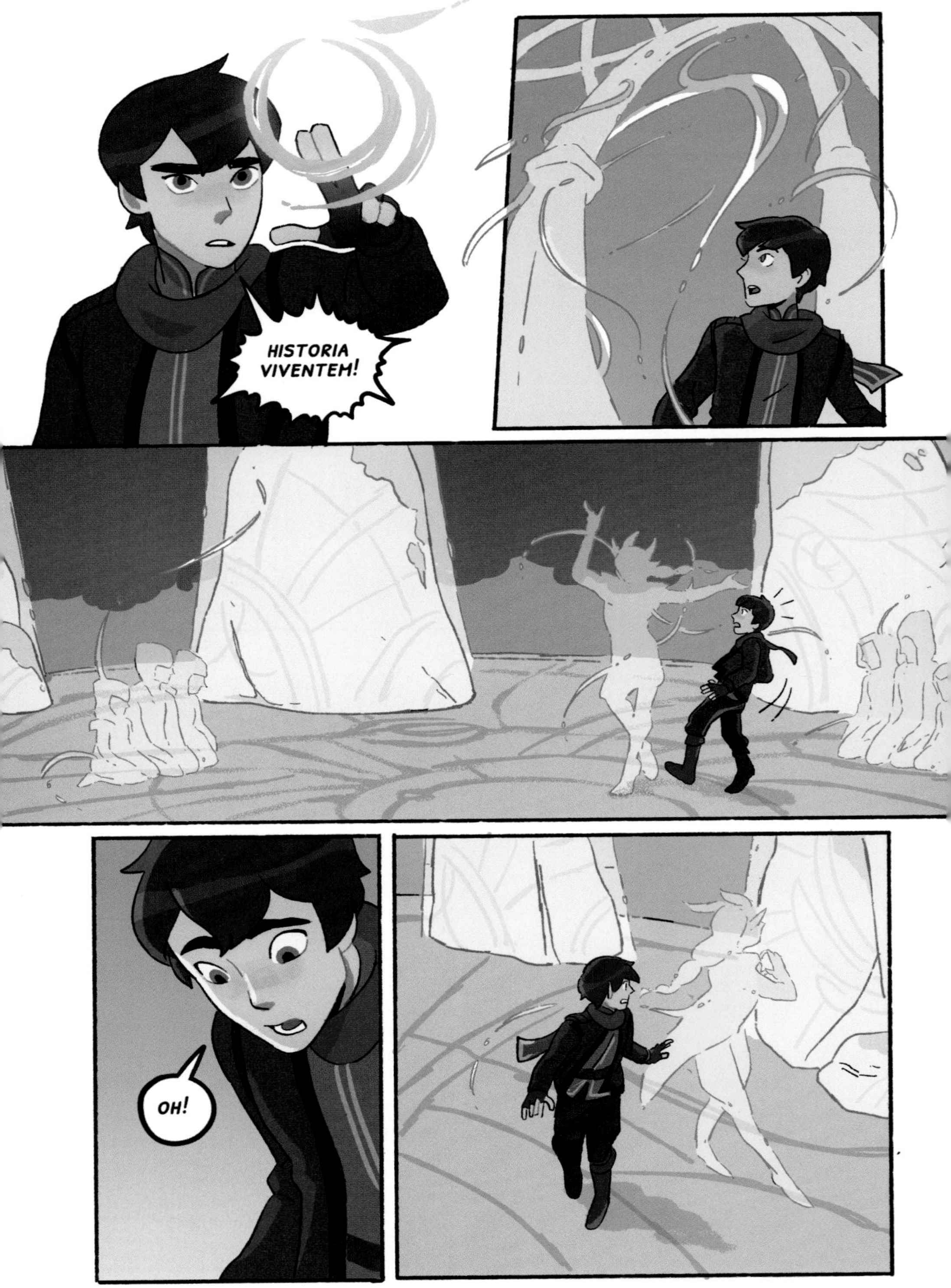
HISTORIA VIVENTEM!
OH!

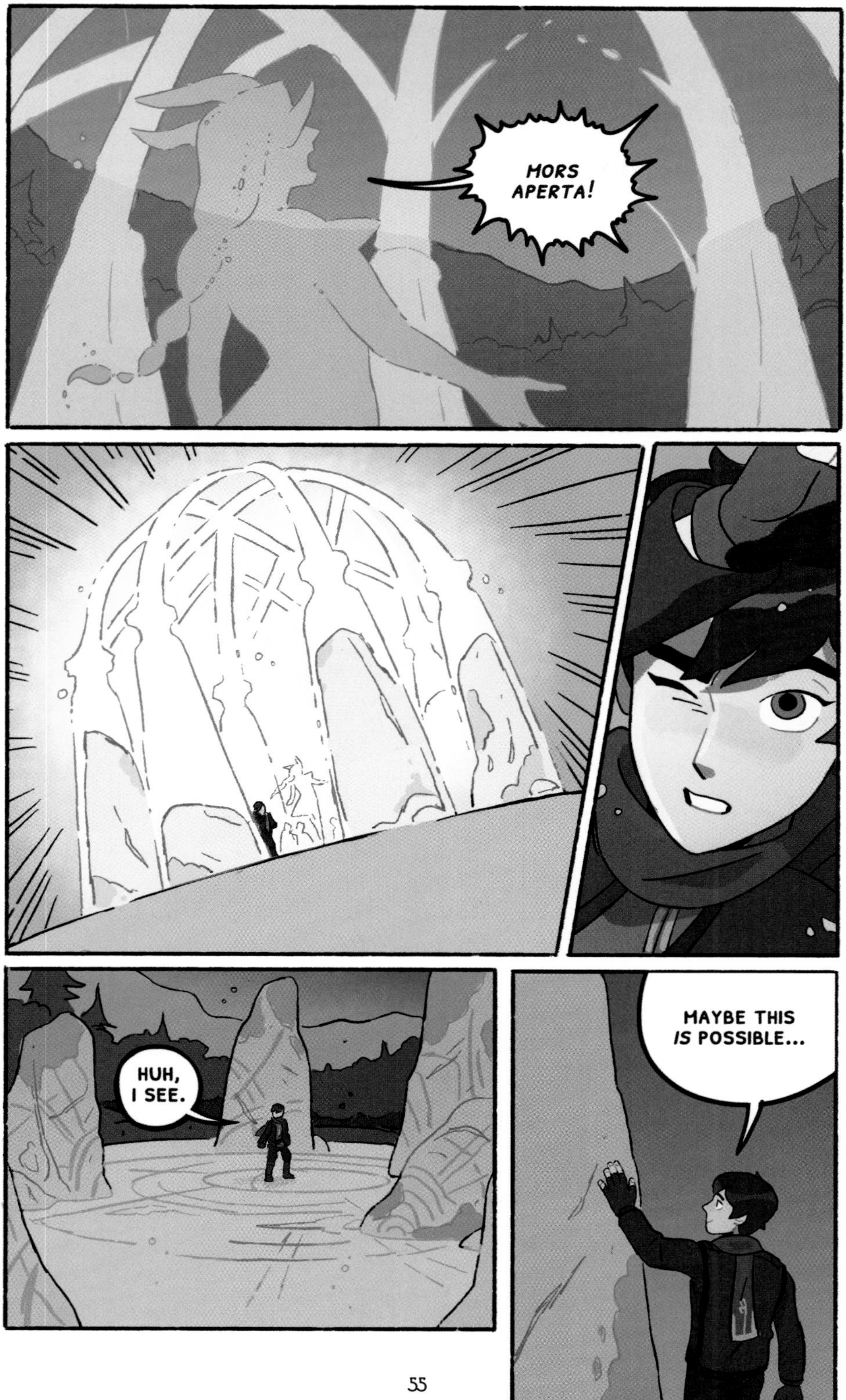
MORS APERTA!
HUH, I SEE.
MAYBE THIS IS POSSIBLE...

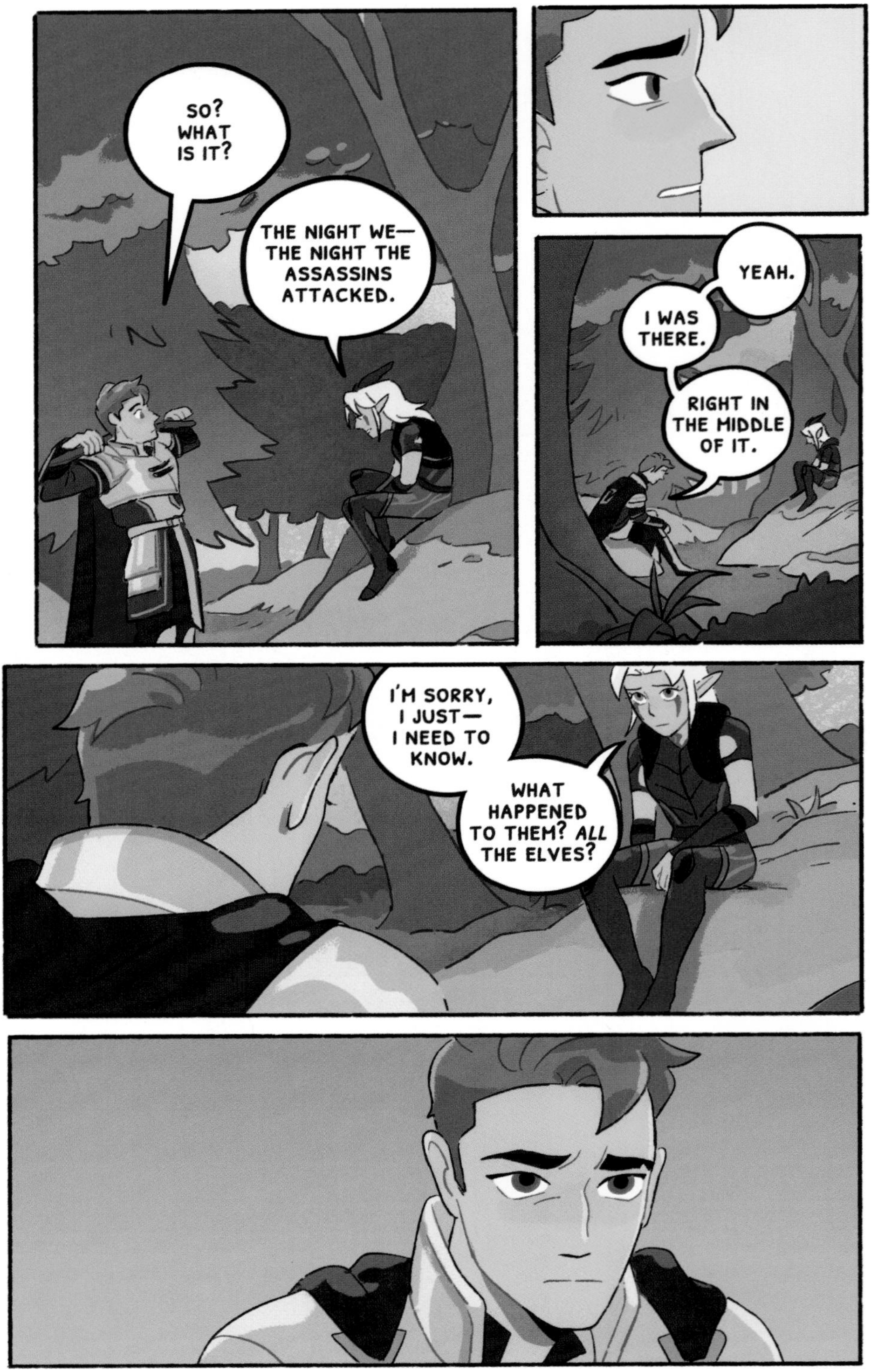
SO? WHAT IS IT?
THE NIGHT WE— THE NIGHT THE ASSASSINS ATTACKED.
YEAH.
I WAS THERE.
RIGHT IN THE MIDDLE OF IT.
I'M SORRY, I JUST— I NEED TO KNOW.
WHAT HAPPENED TO THEM? *ALL* THE ELVES?

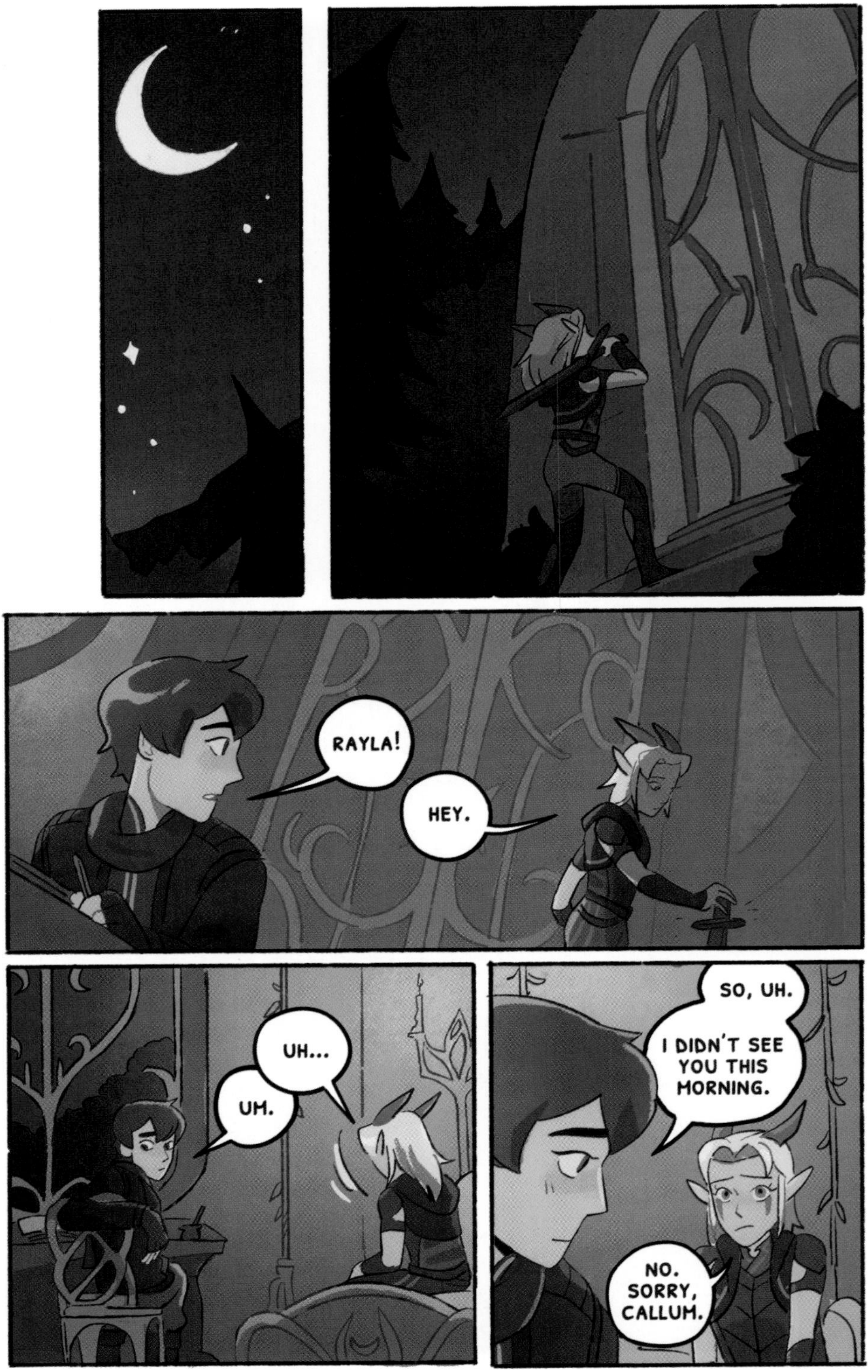
RAYLA!
HEY.
UM.
UH...
SO, UH.
I DIDN'T SEE YOU THIS MORNING.
NO. SORRY, CALLUM.

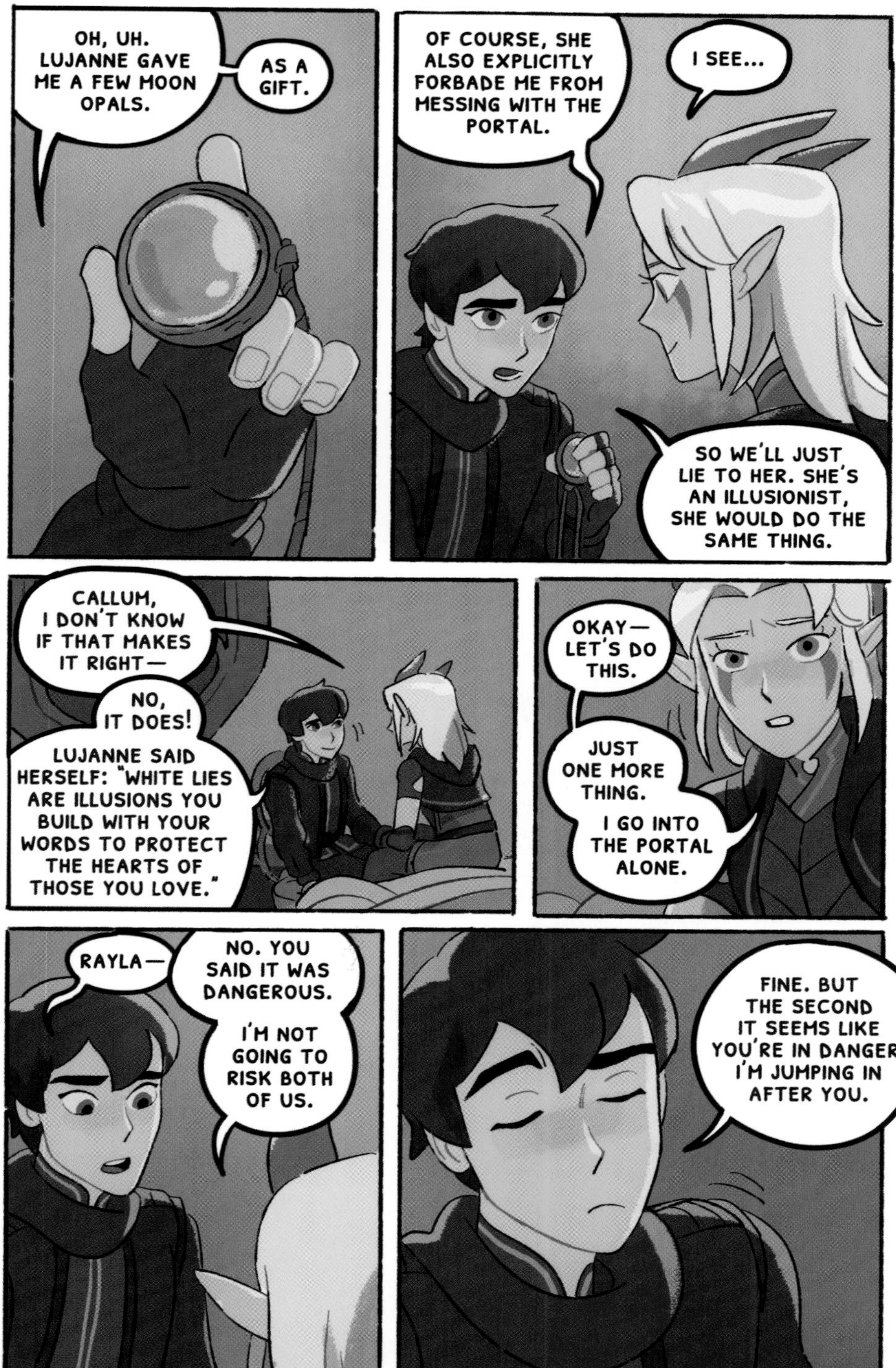
OH, UH. LUJANNE GAVE ME A FEW MOON OPALS.
AS A GIFT.
OF COURSE, SHE ALSO EXPLICITLY FORBADE ME FROM MESSING WITH THE PORTAL.
I SEE...
SO WE'LL JUST LIE TO HER. SHE'S AN ILLUSIONIST, SHE WOULD DO THE SAME THING.
CALLUM, I DON'T KNOW IF THAT MAKES IT RIGHT—
NO, IT DOES!
LUJANNE SAID HERSELF: "WHITE LIES ARE ILLUSIONS YOU BUILD WITH YOUR WORDS TO PROTECT THE HEARTS OF THOSE YOU LOVE."
OKAY— LET'S DO THIS.
JUST ONE MORE THING.
I GO INTO THE PORTAL ALONE.
RAYLA—
NO. YOU SAID IT WAS DANGEROUS.
I'M NOT GOING TO RISK BOTH OF US.
FINE. BUT THE SECOND IT SEEMS LIKE YOU'RE IN DANGER, I'M JUMPING IN AFTER YOU.

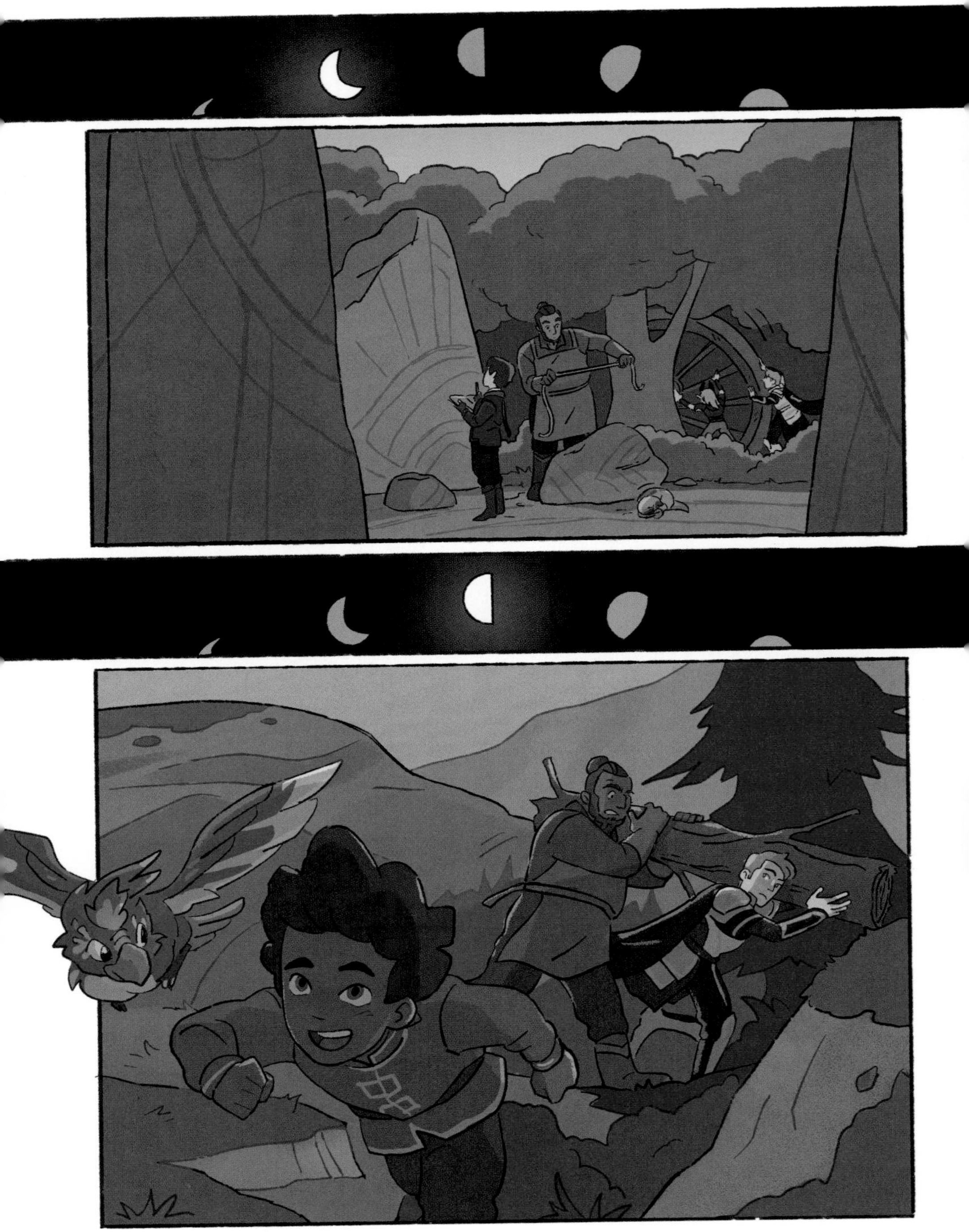

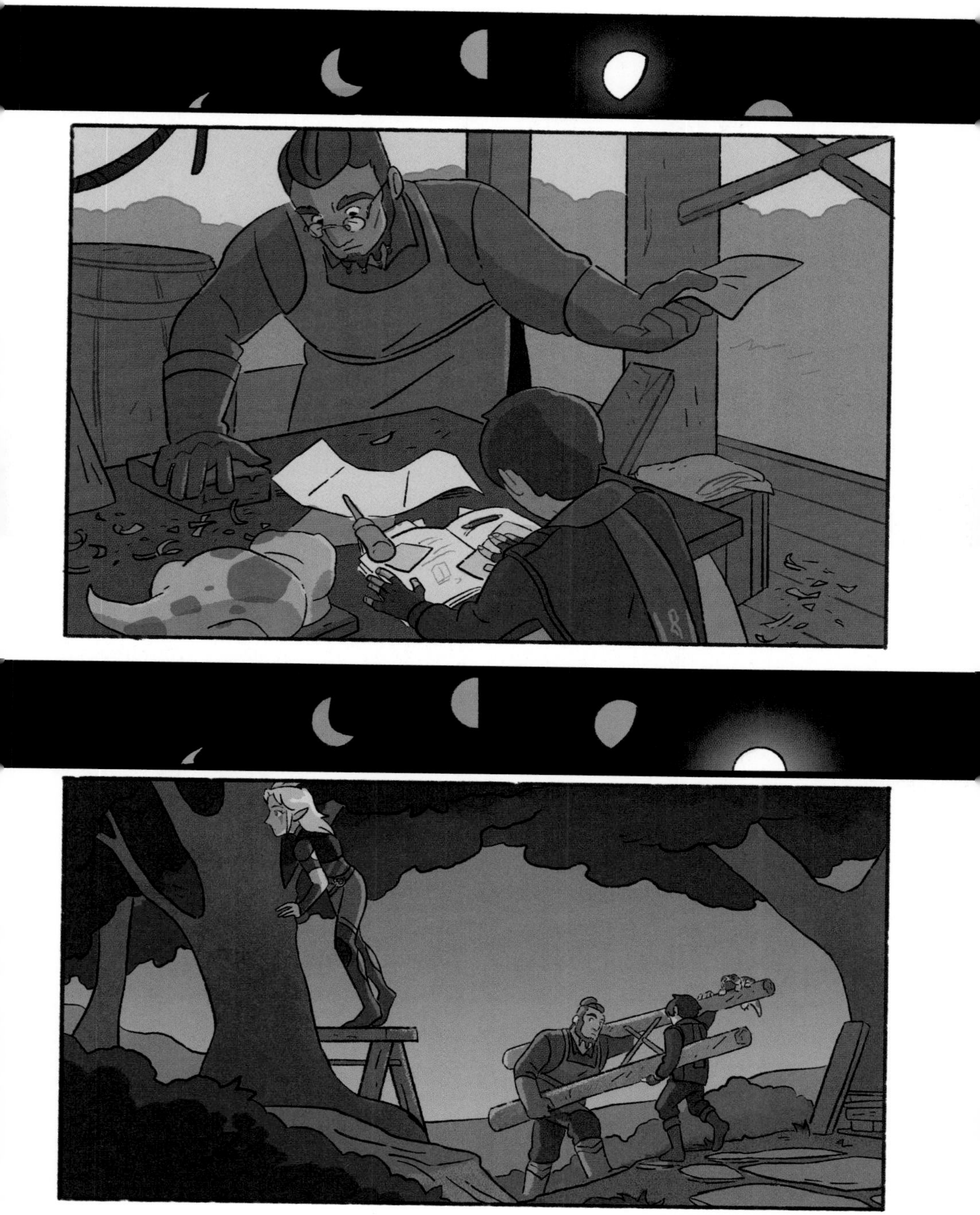

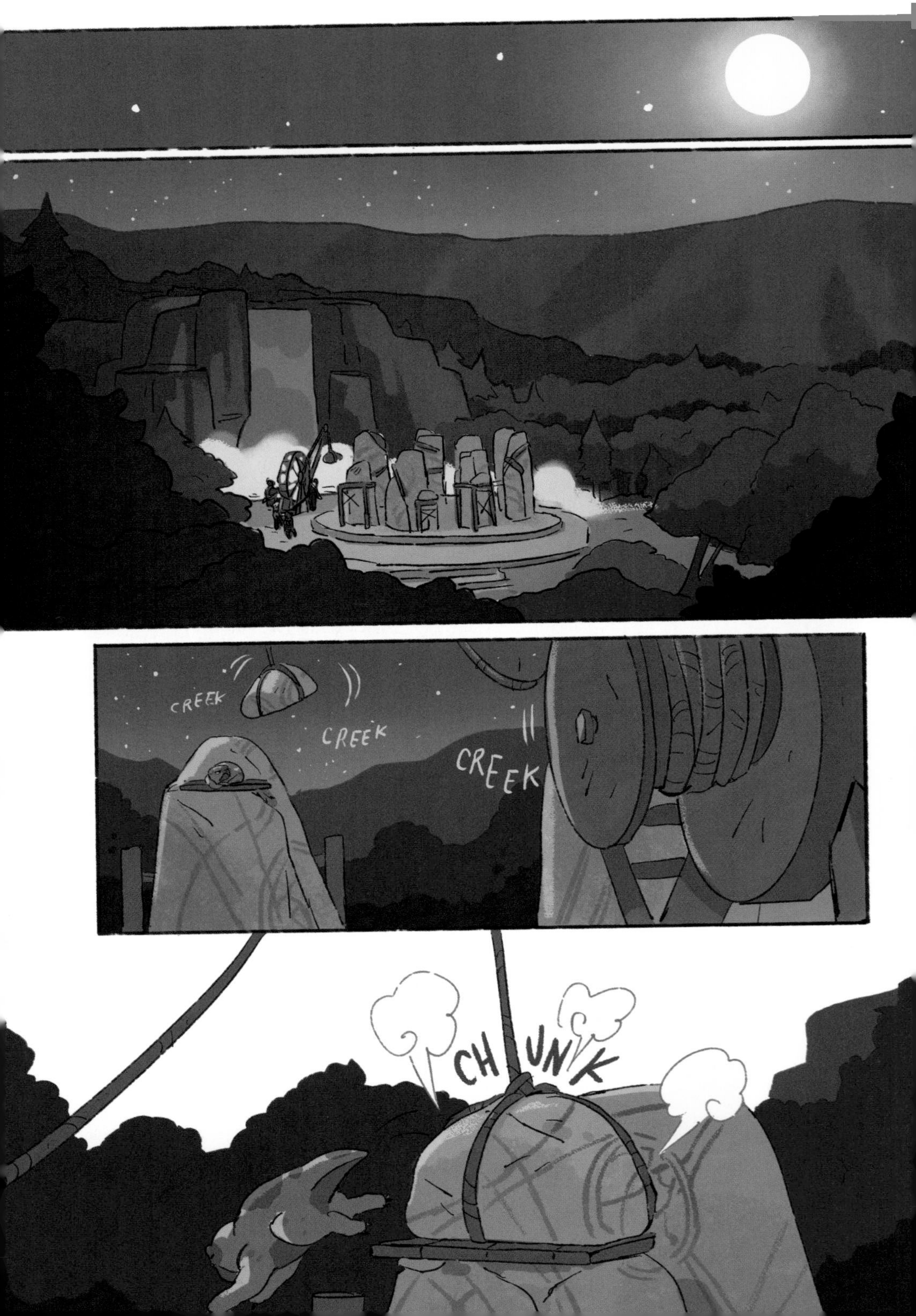
CREEK
CREEK
CREEK
CHUNK

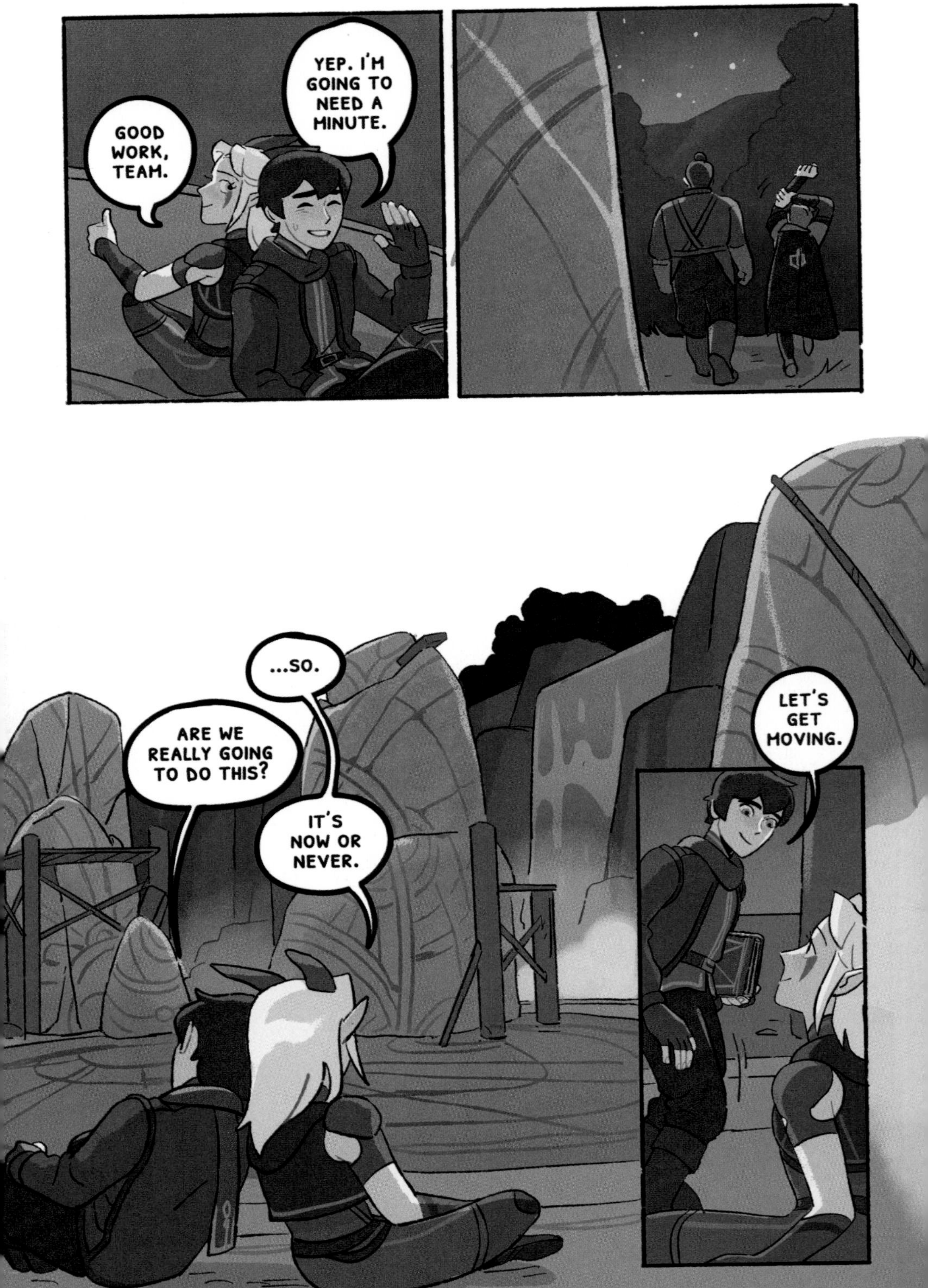
GOOD WORK, TEAM.
YEP. I'M GOING TO NEED A MINUTE.
...SO.
ARE WE REALLY GOING TO DO THIS?
IT'S NOW OR NEVER.
LET'S GET MOVING.

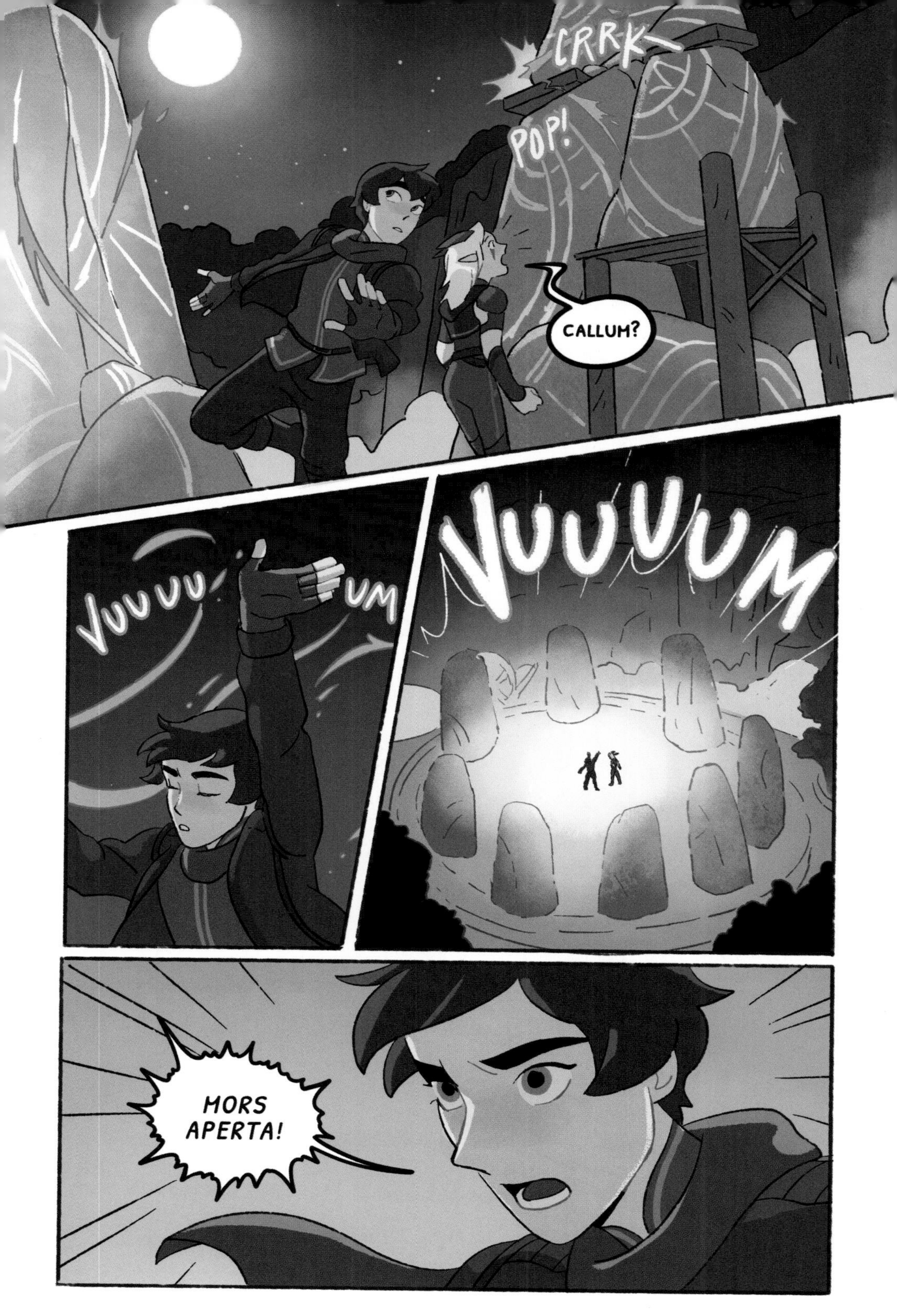
CRRK
POP!
CALLUM?
VUUUU UM
VUUUUM
MORS APERTA!

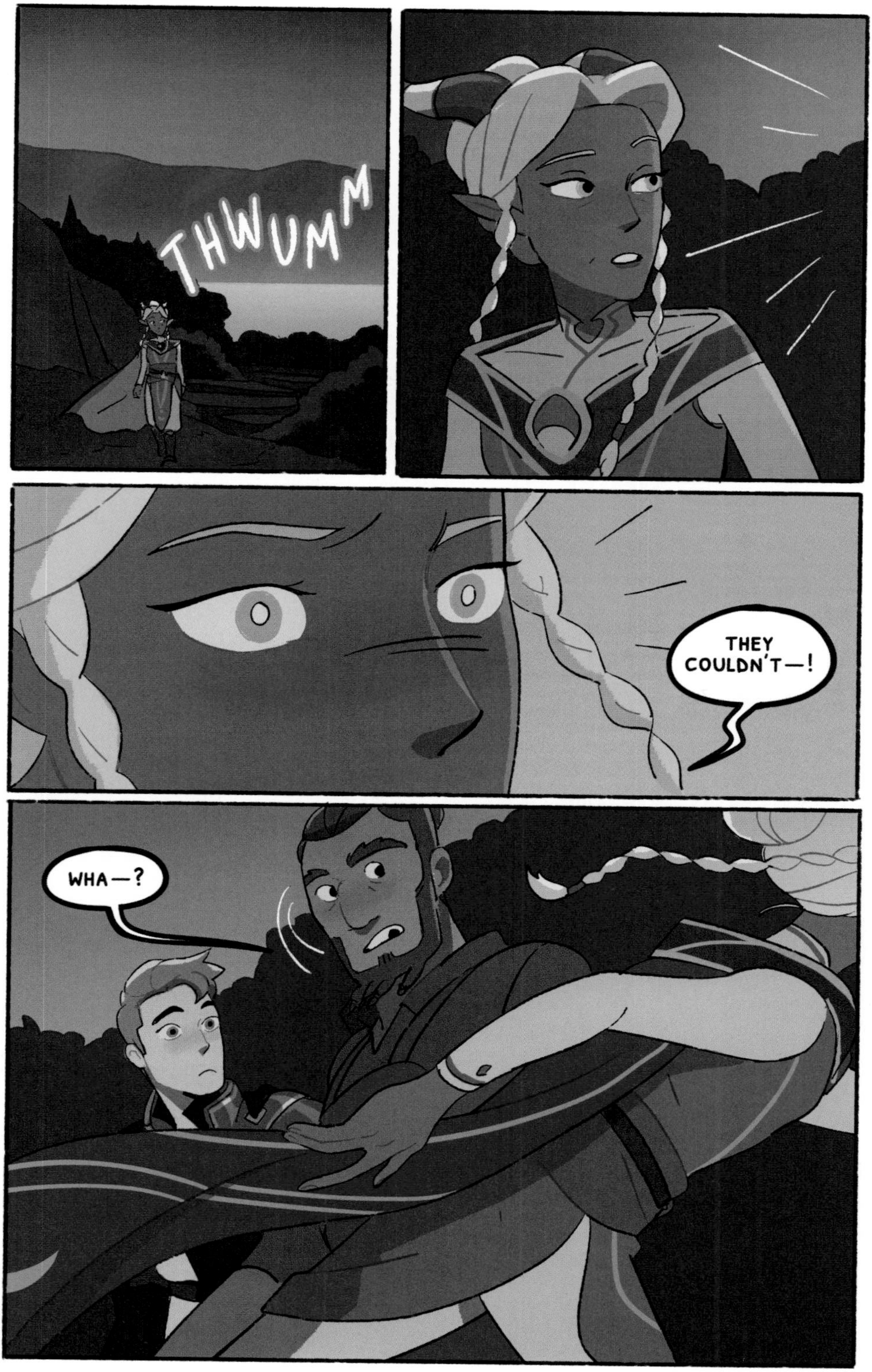
THWUMM
THEY COULDN'T—!
WHA—?

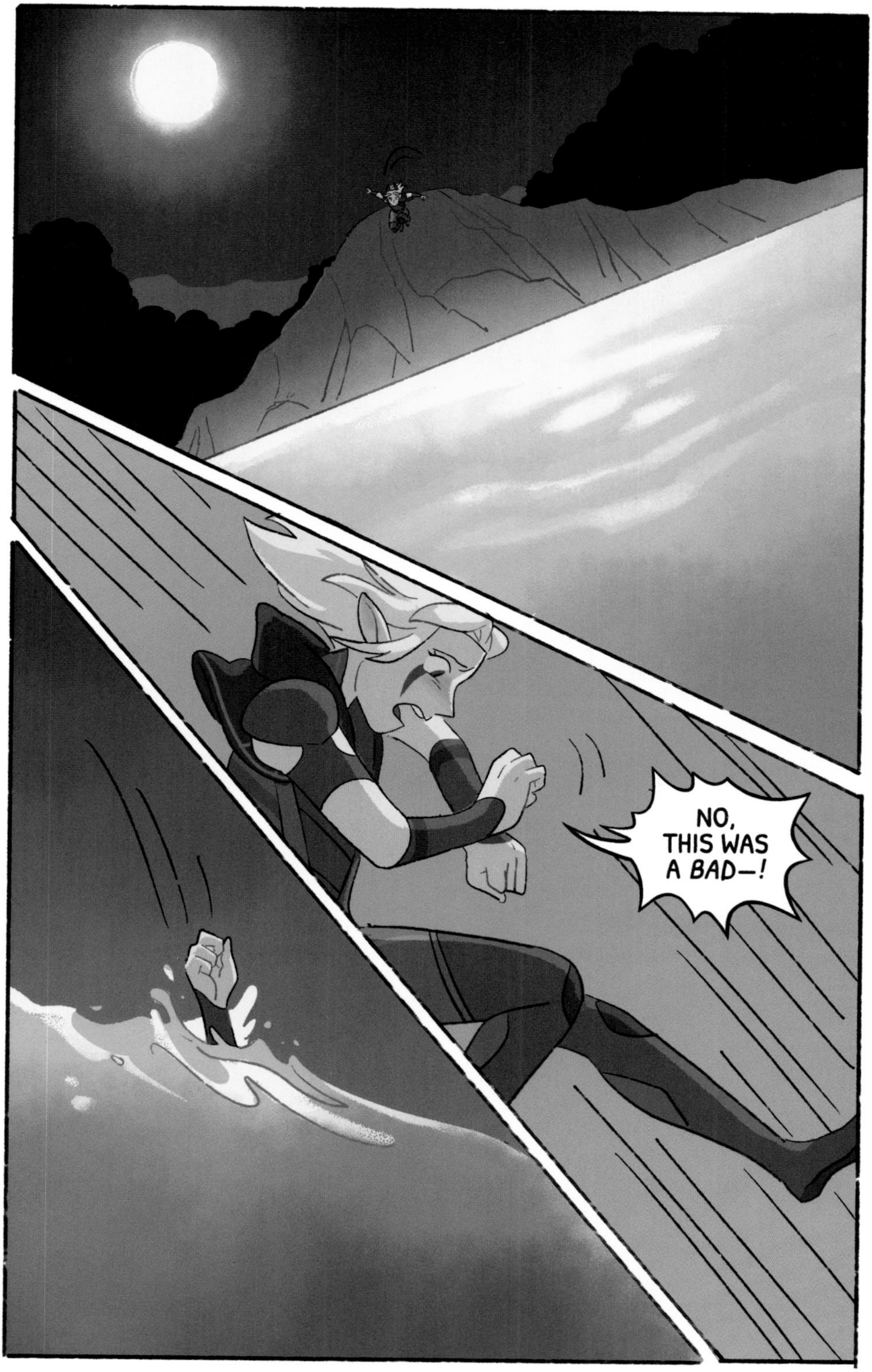
NO, THIS WAS A BAD—!

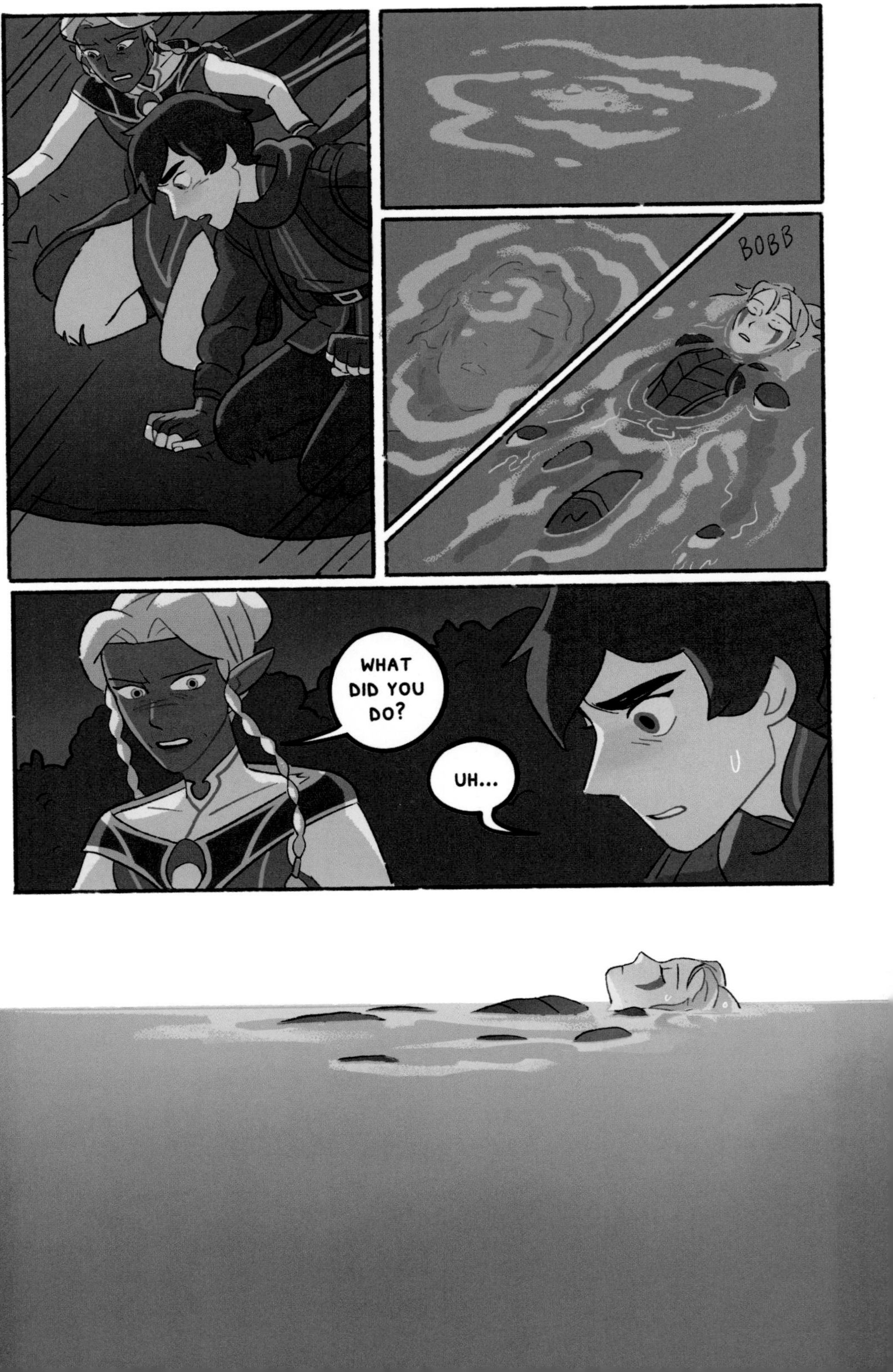
BOBB
WHAT DID YOU DO?
UH...

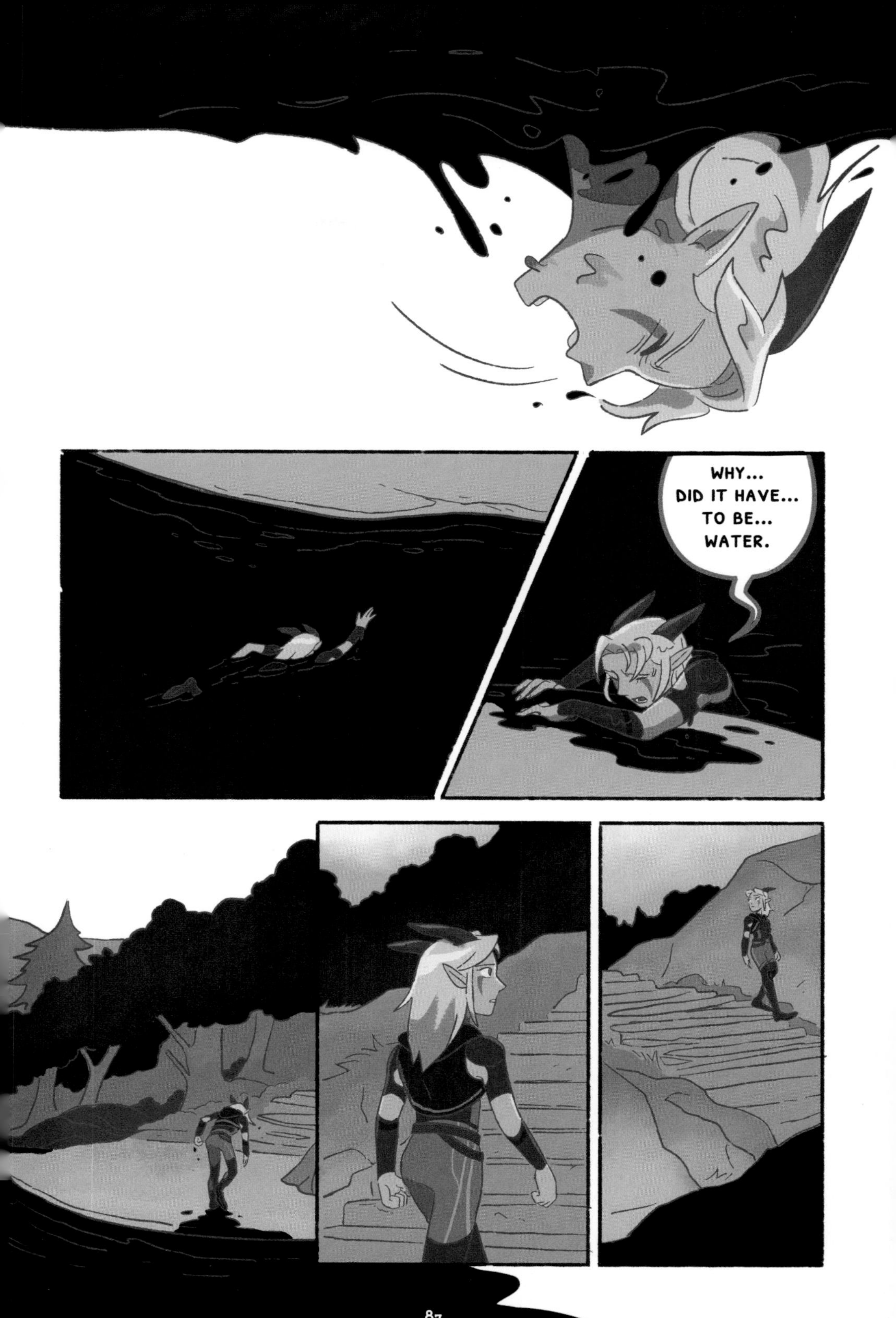
WHY...
DID IT HAVE...
TO BE...
WATER.

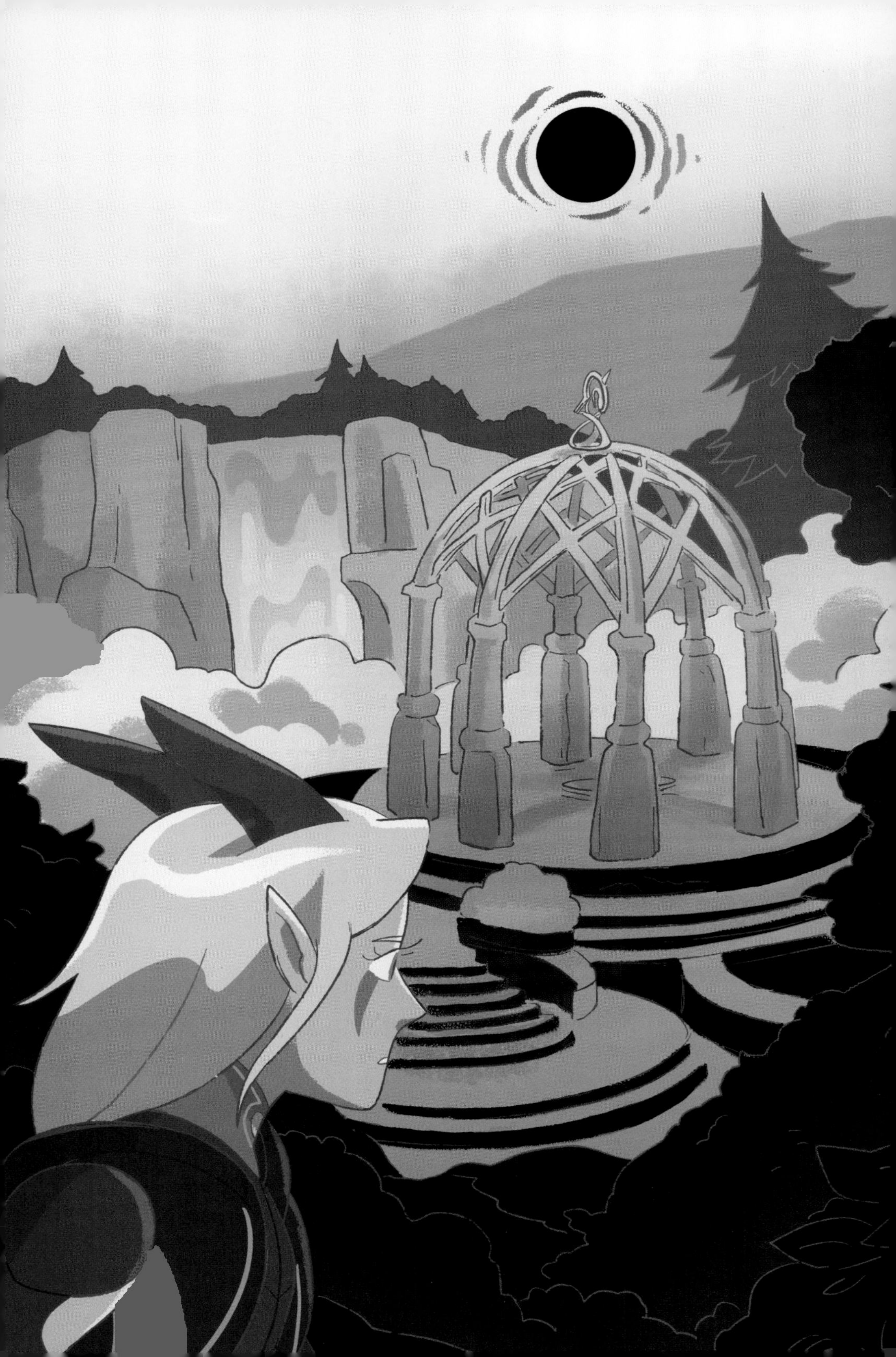

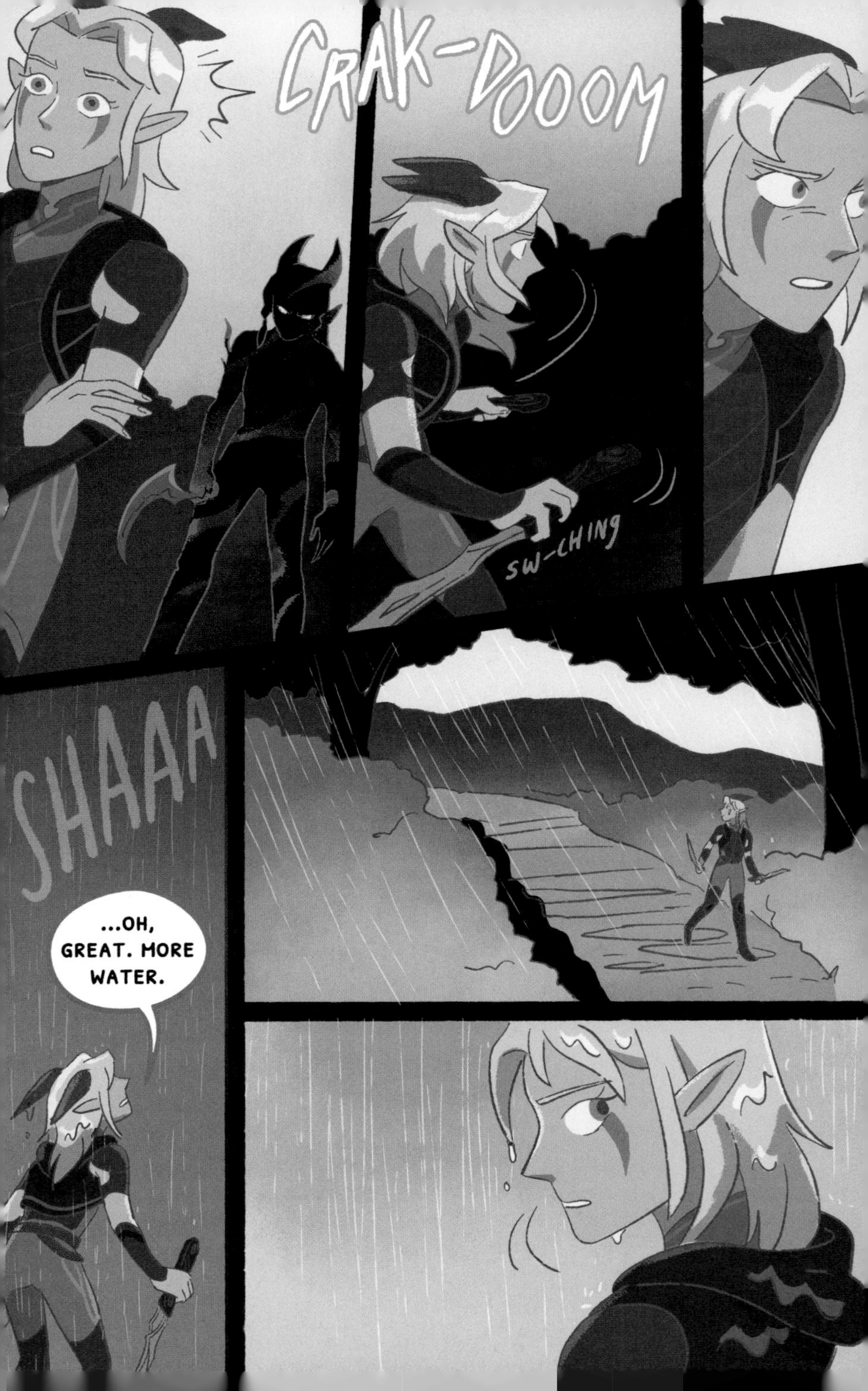
CRAK-DOOOM
SW-CHING
SHAAA
...OH, GREAT. MORE WATER.

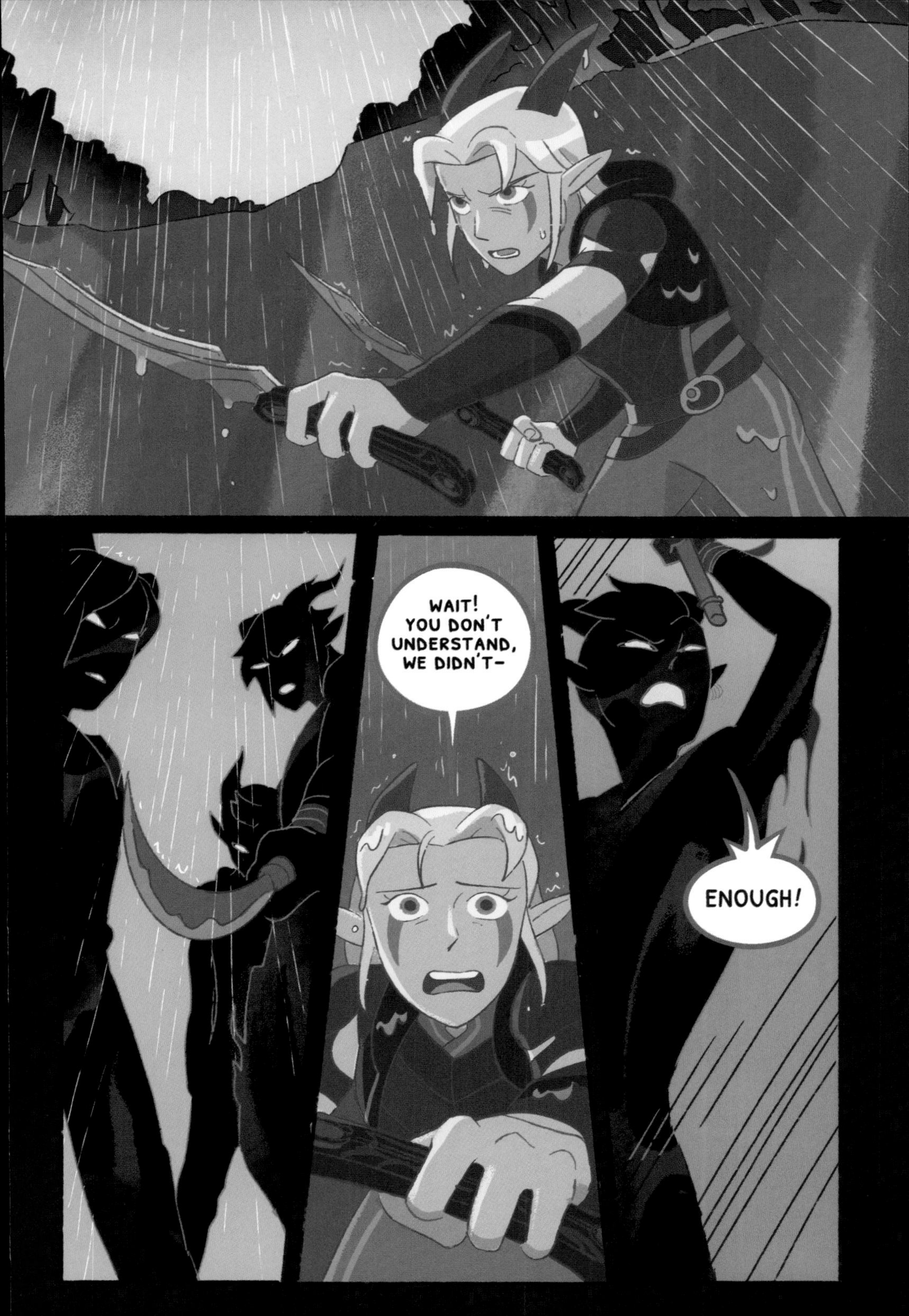
WAIT! YOU DON'T UNDERSTAND, WE DIDN'T-
ENOUGH!

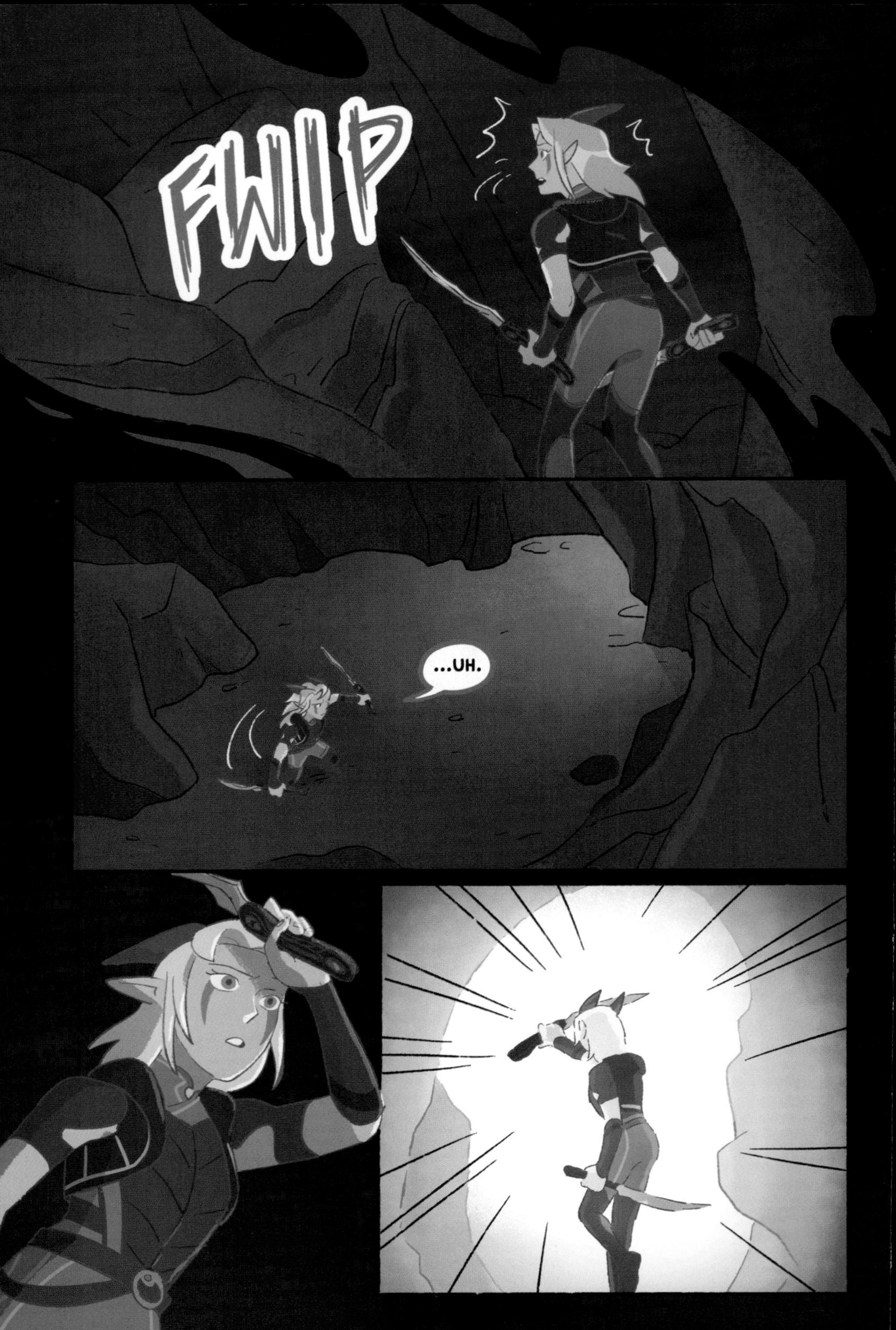
FWIP
...UH.

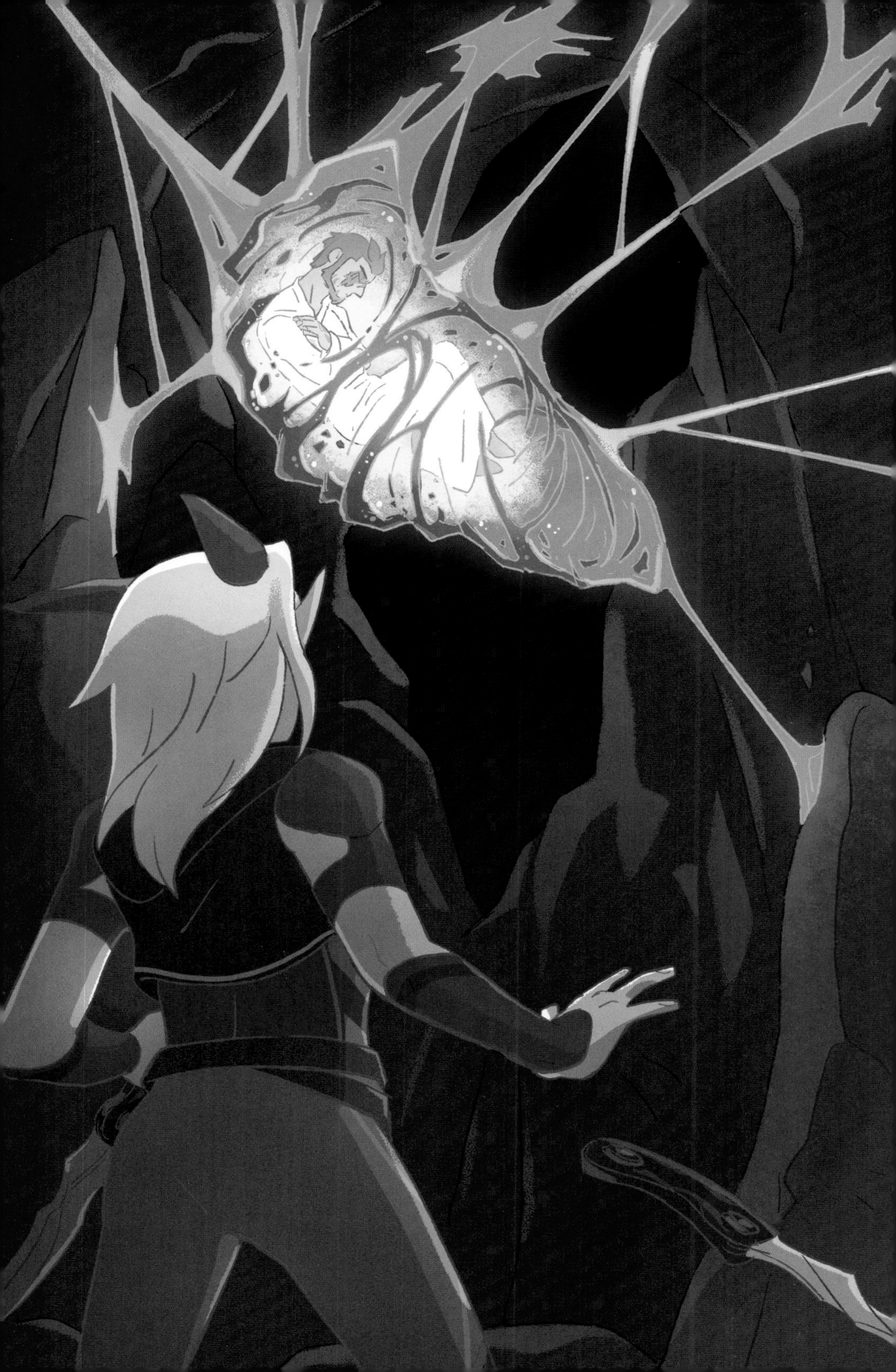

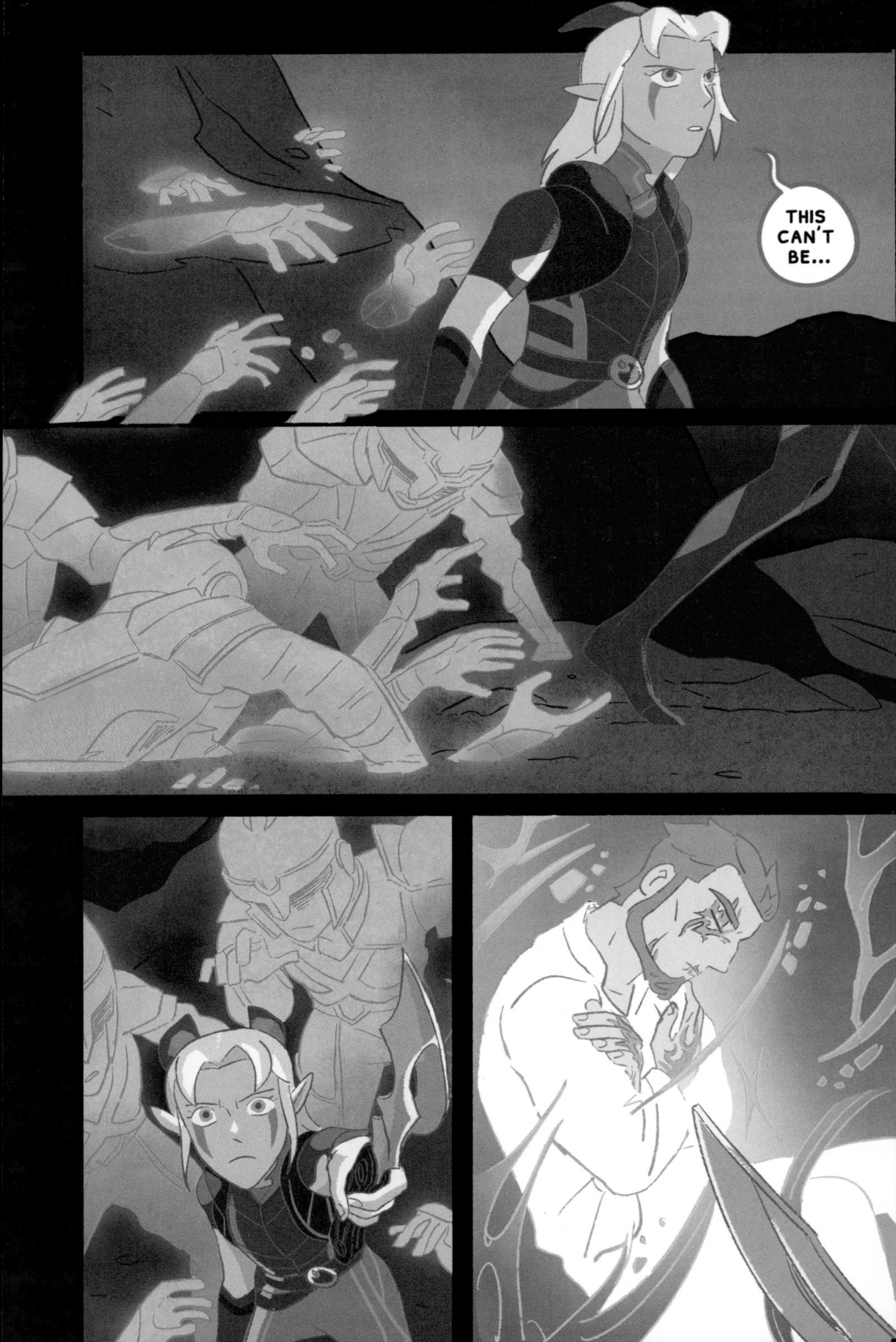
THIS CAN'T BE...

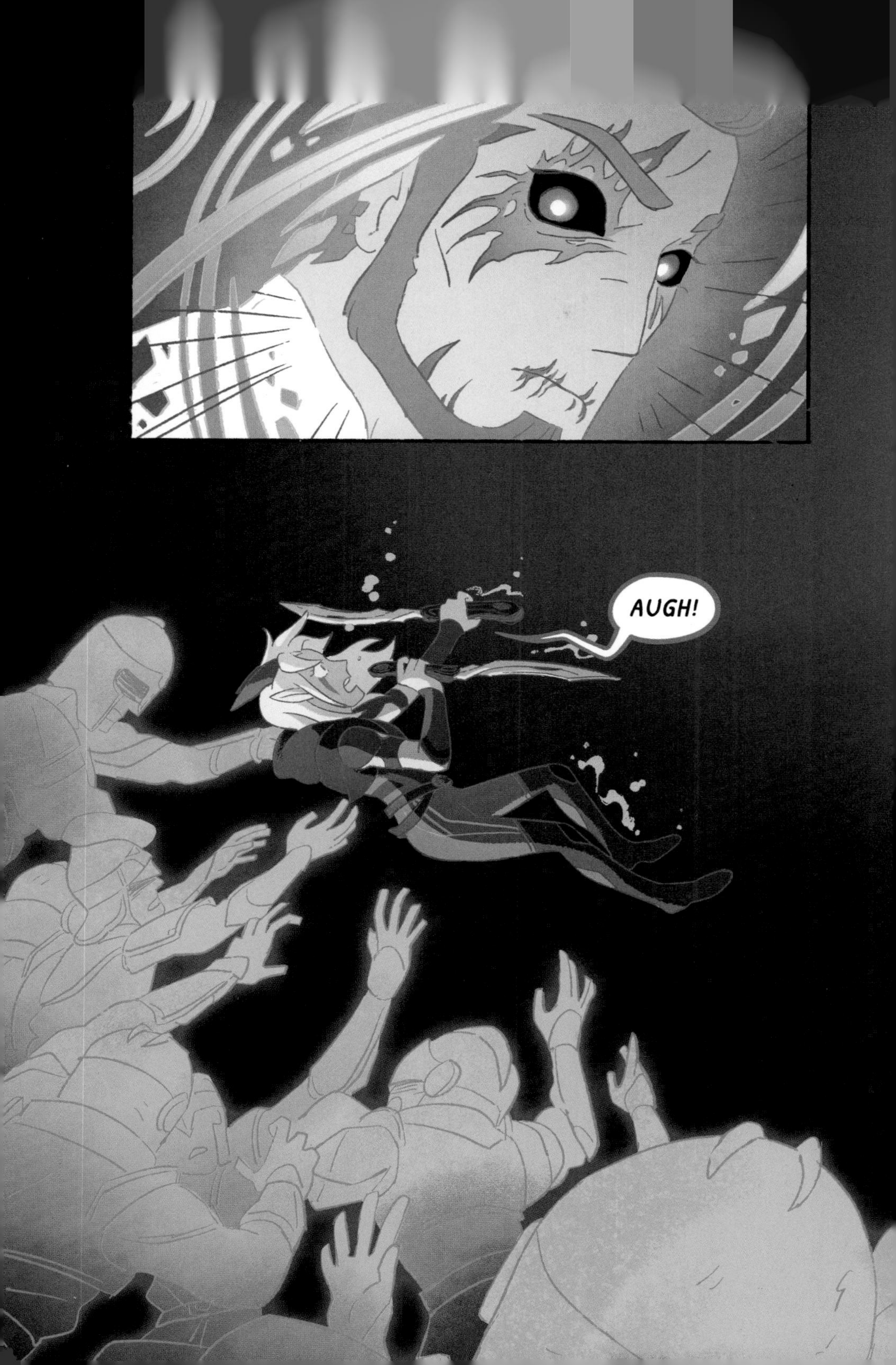
AUGH!

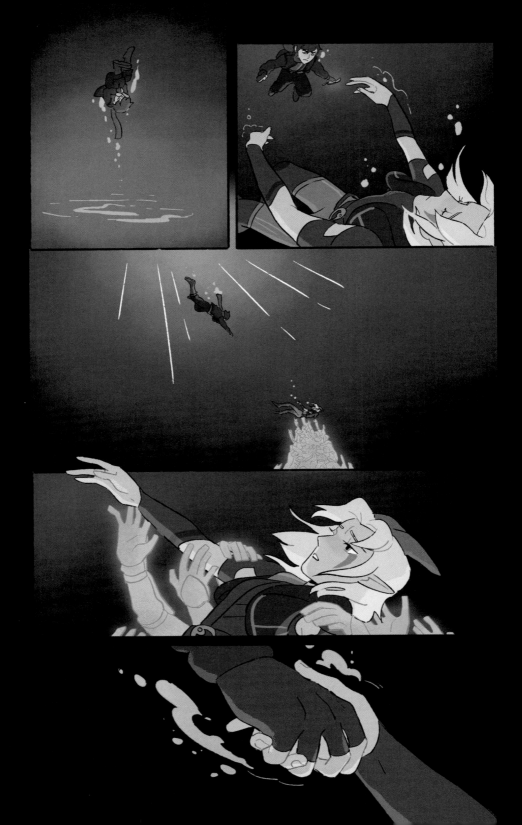

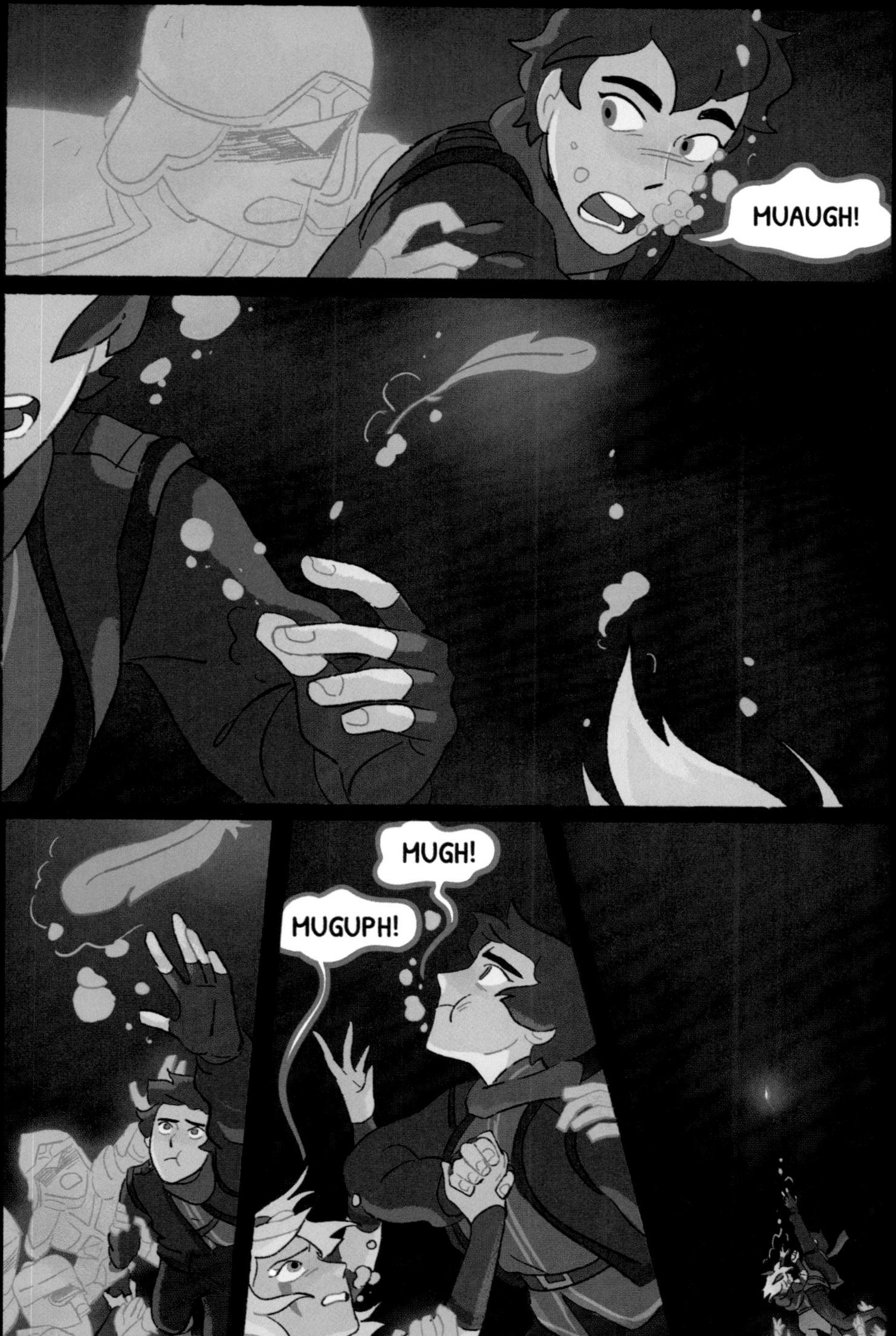
MUAUGH!
MUGH!
MUGUPH!

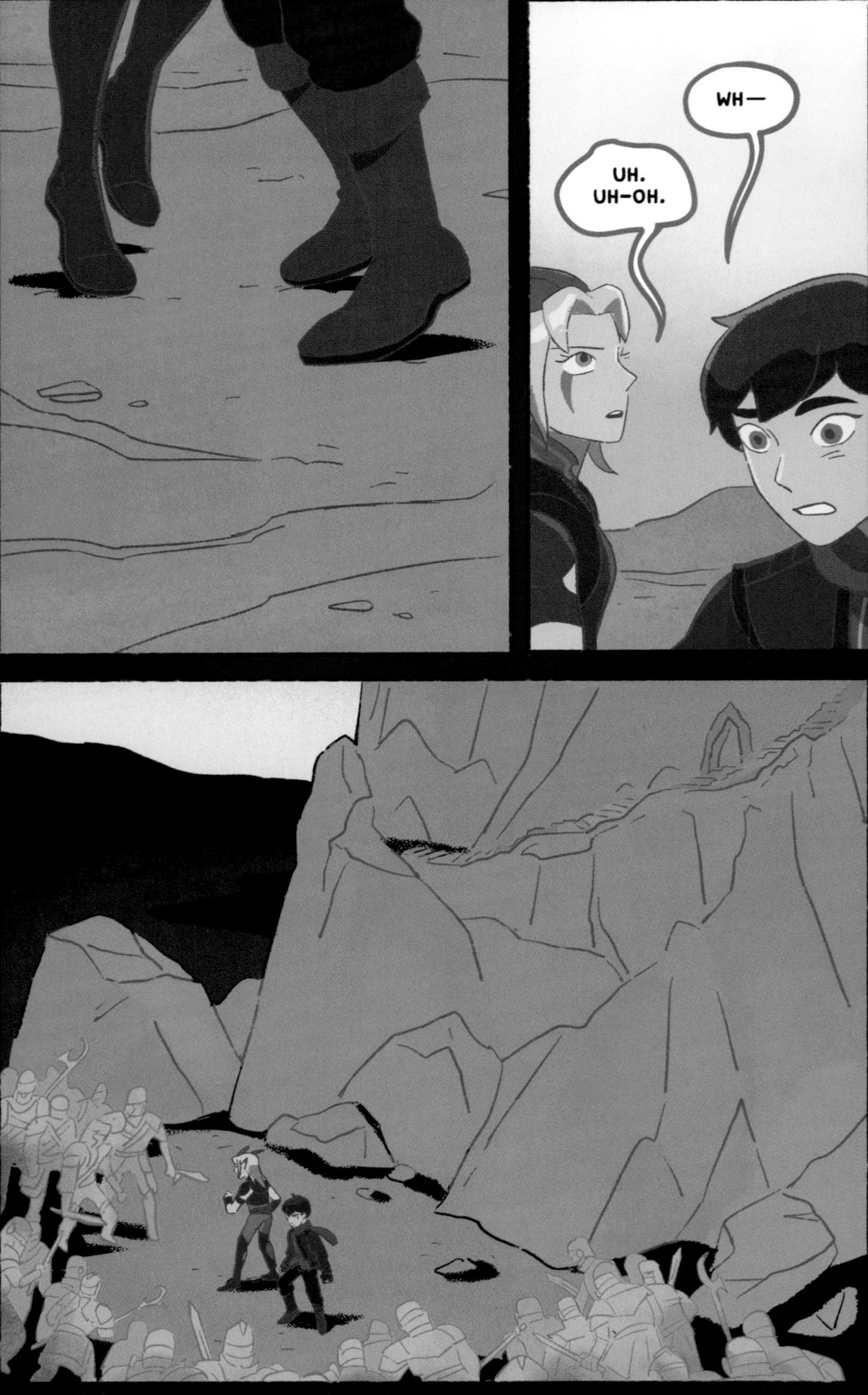
WH—
UH.
UH-OH.

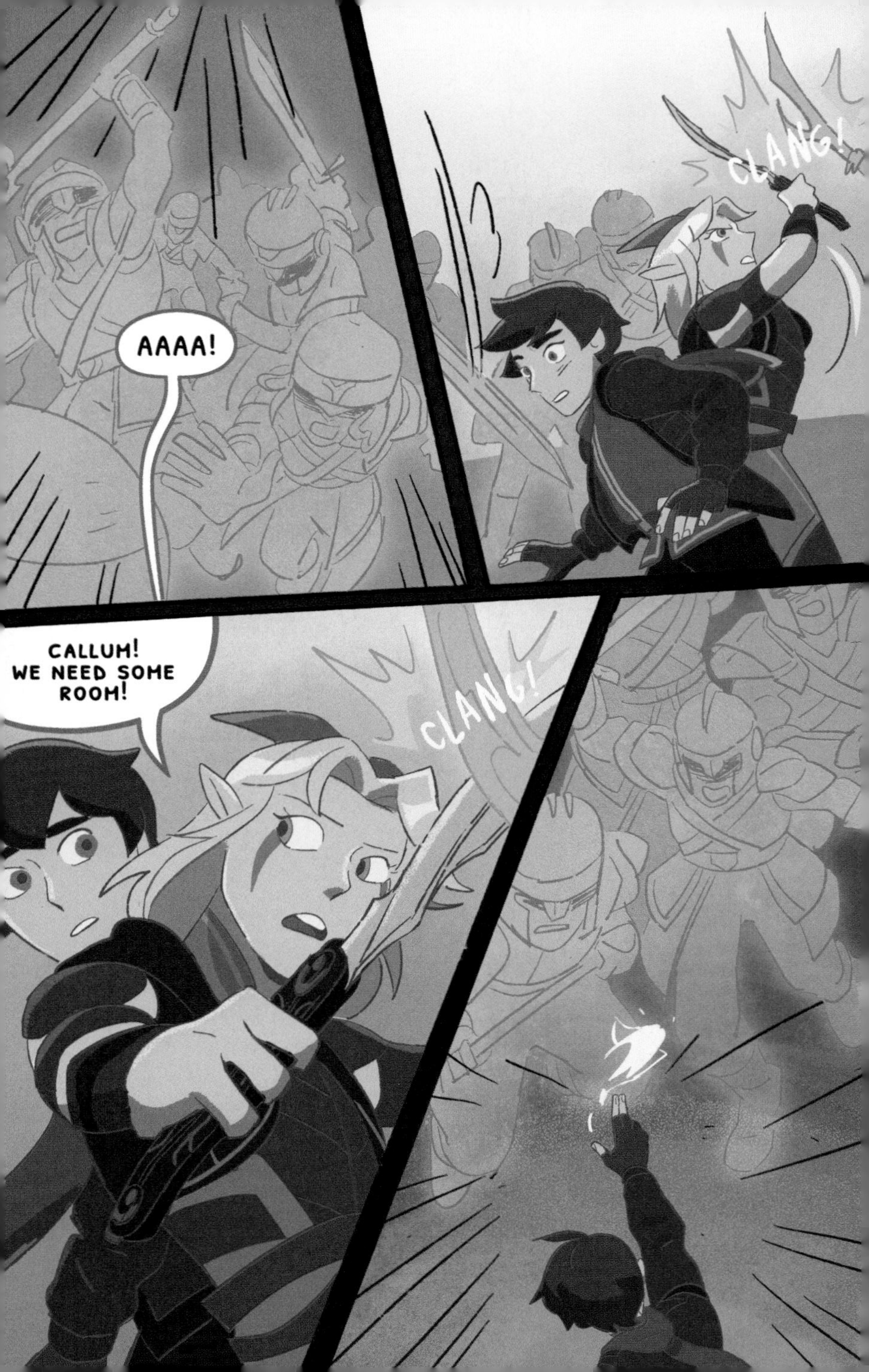
AAAA!
CLANG!
CALLUM! WE NEED SOME ROOM!
CLANG!

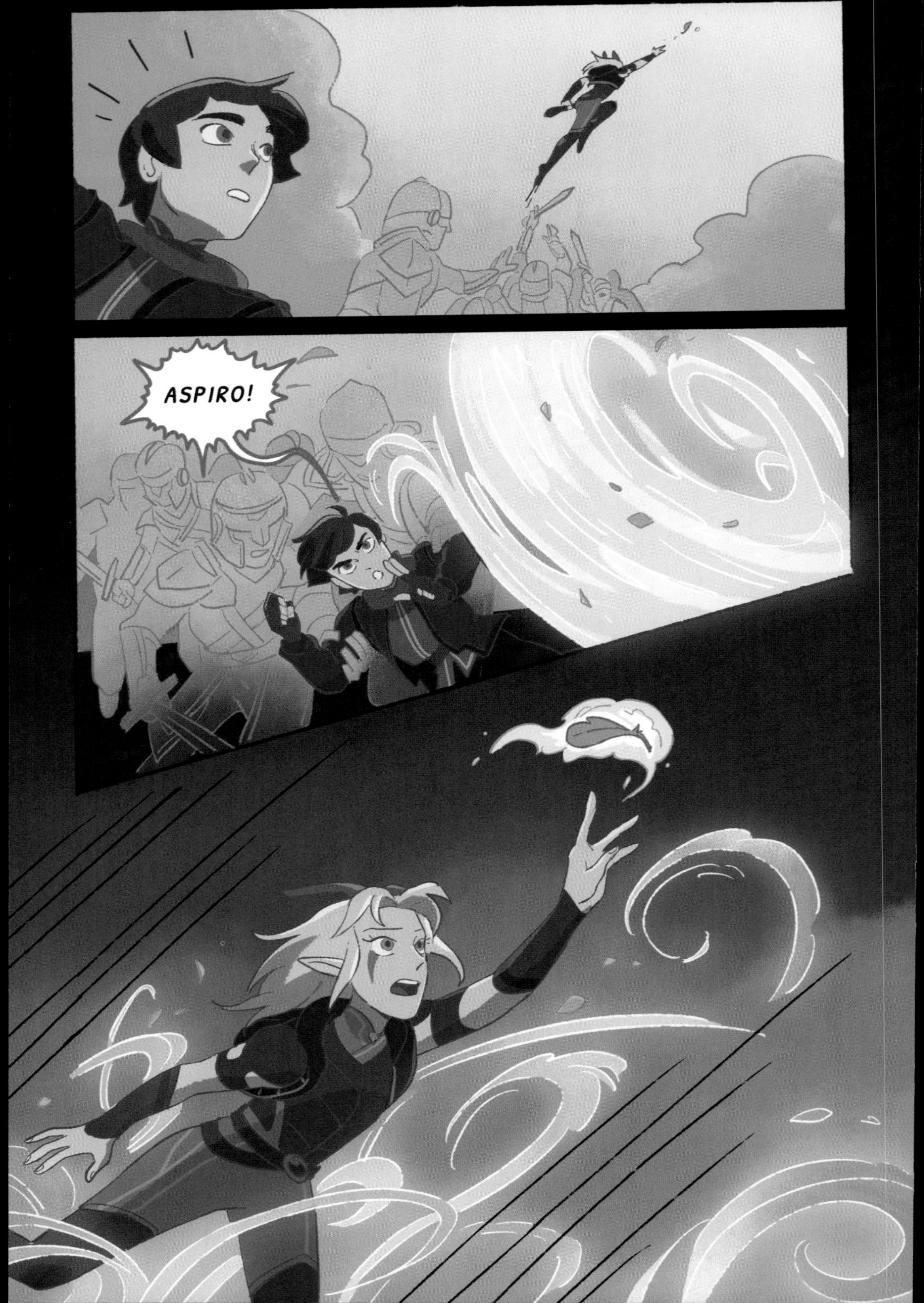
ASPIRO!

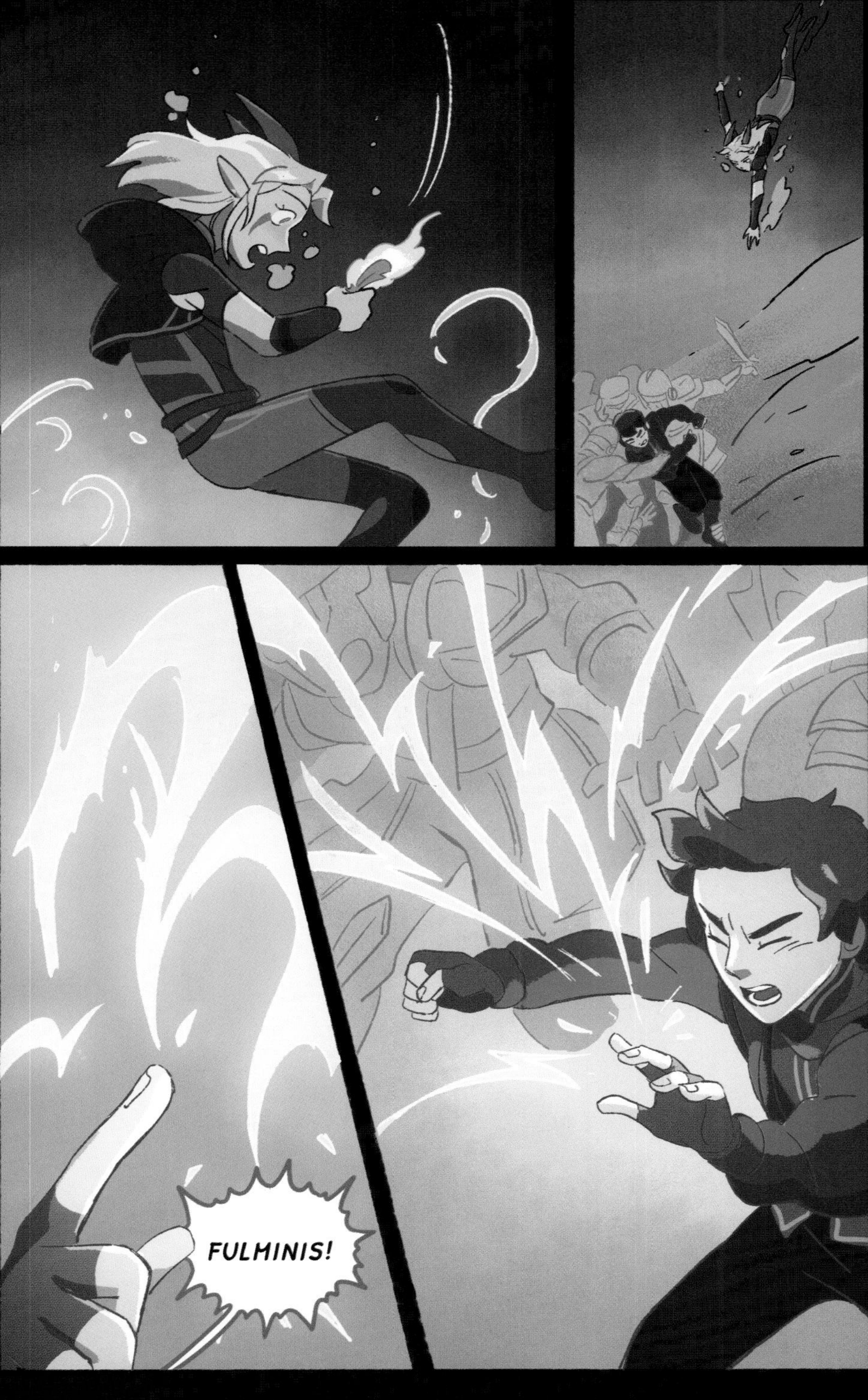
FULMINIS!

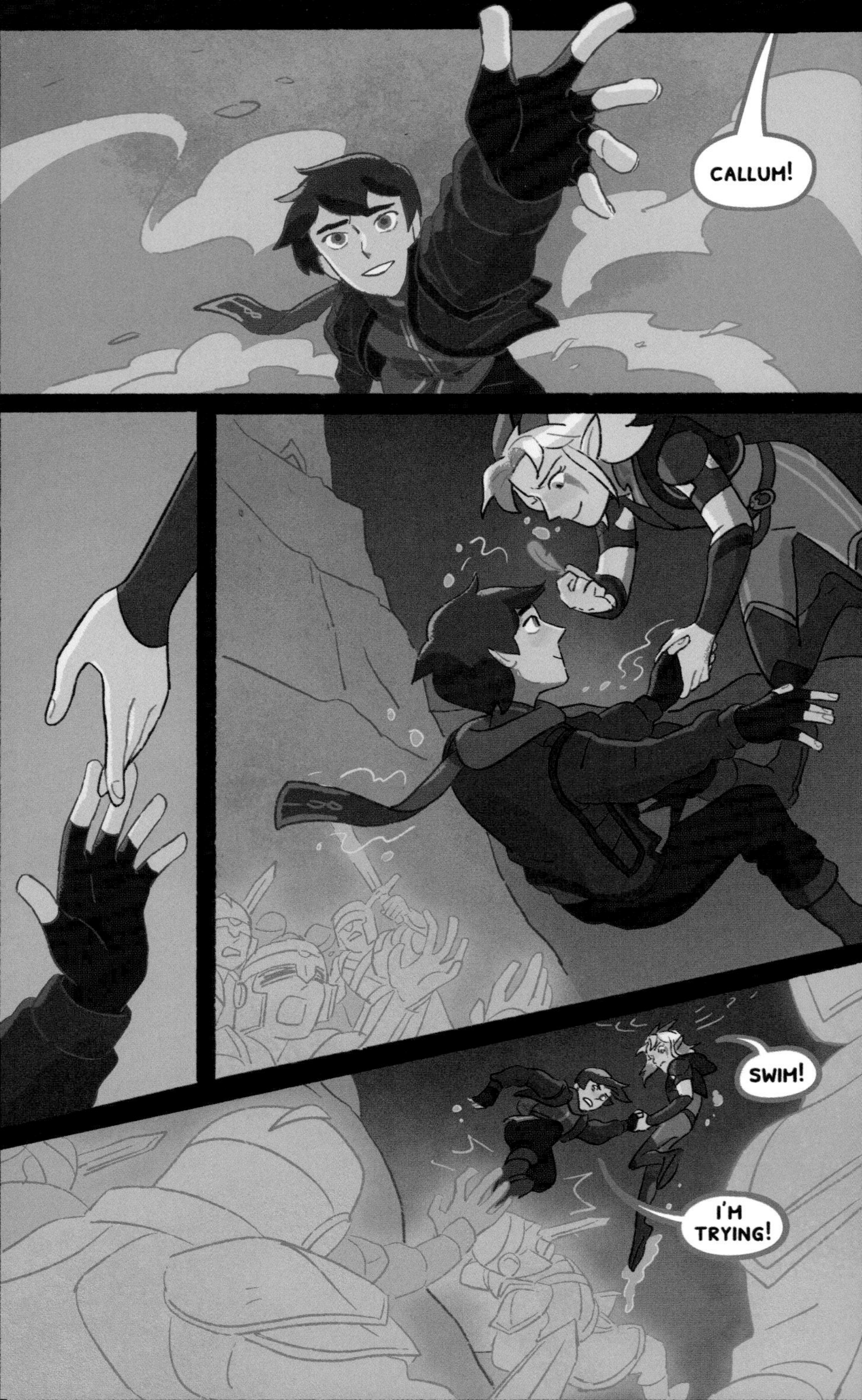
CALLUM!
SWIM!
I'M
TRYING!

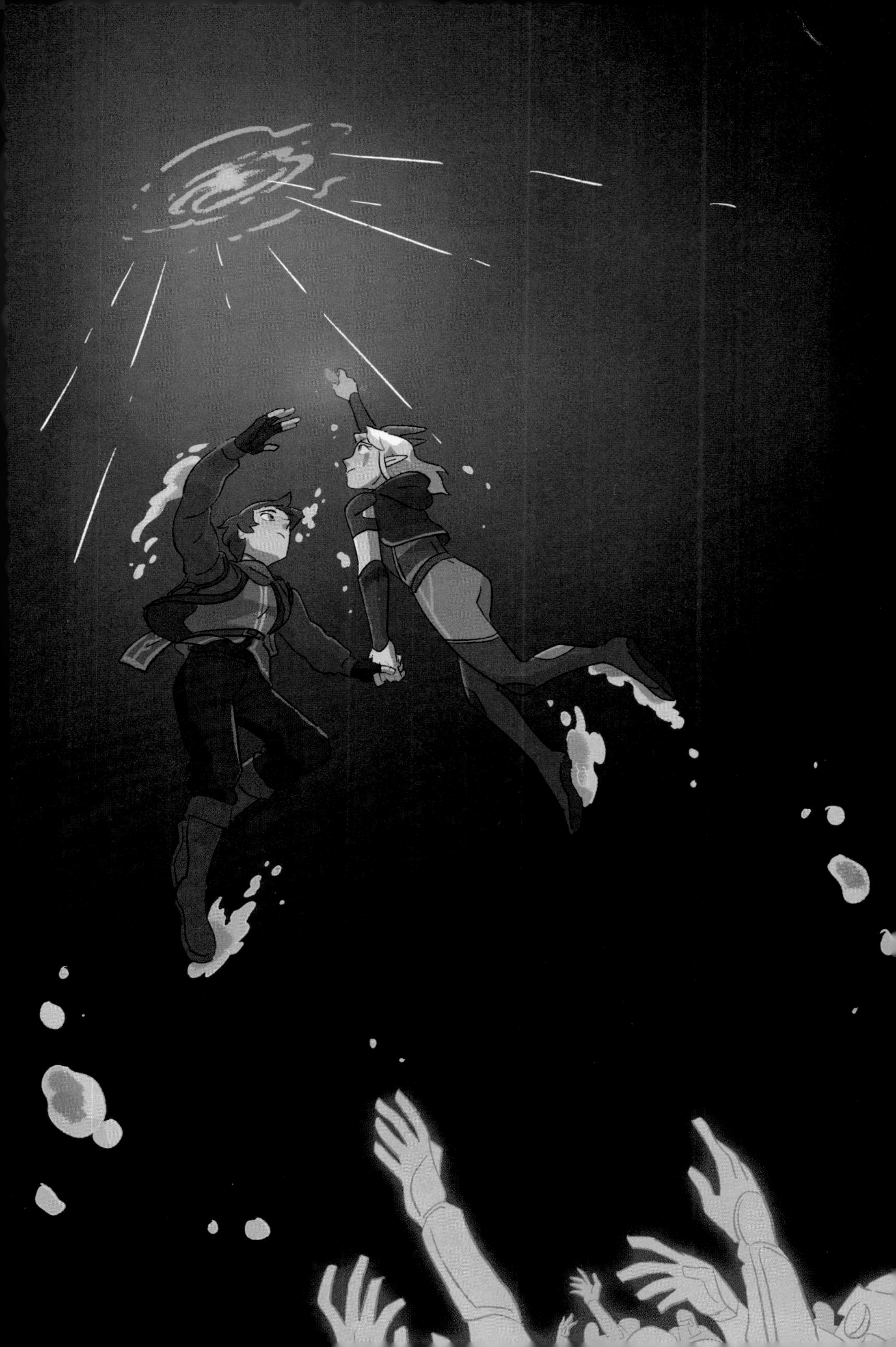

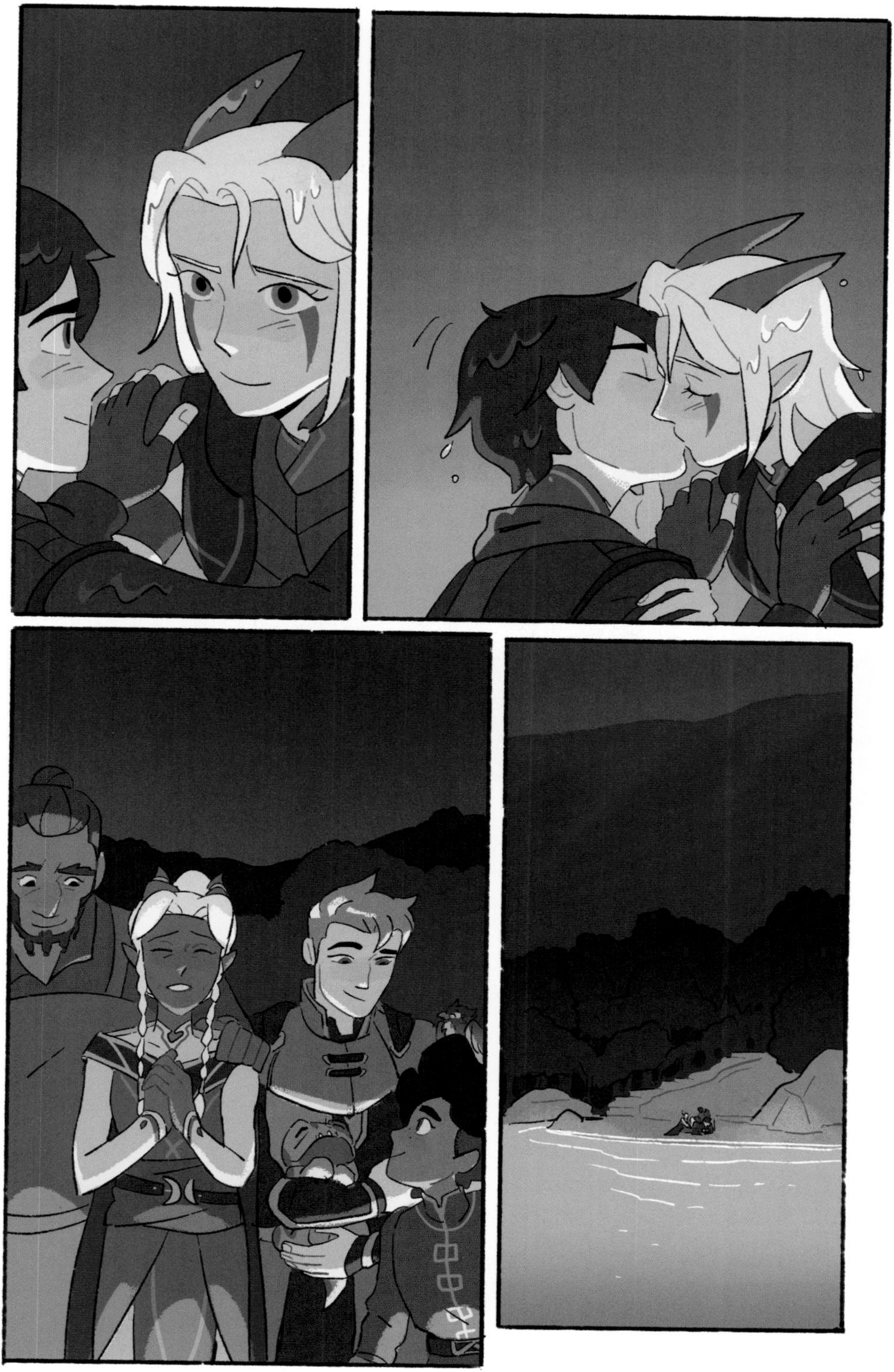

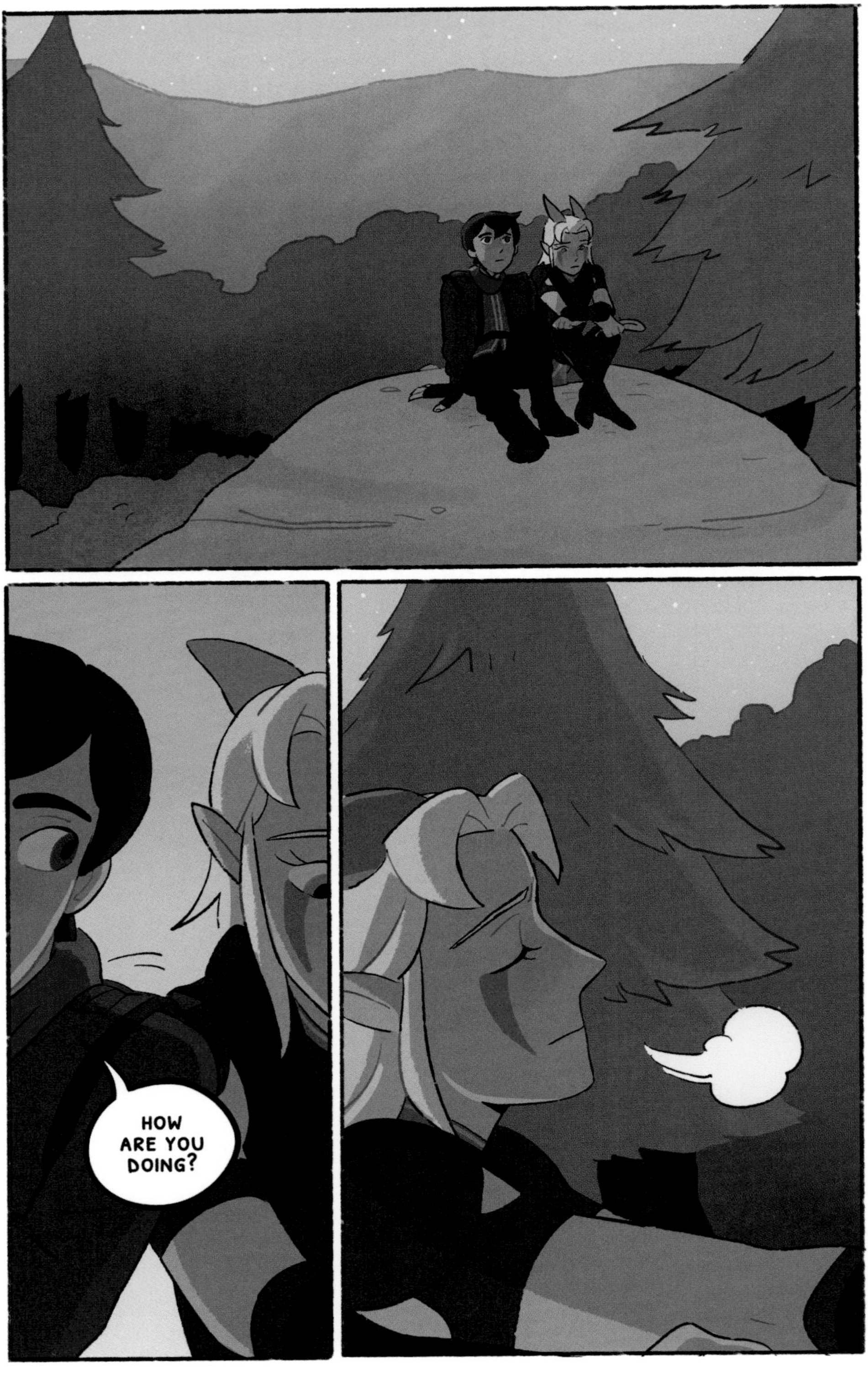
HOW ARE YOU DOING?

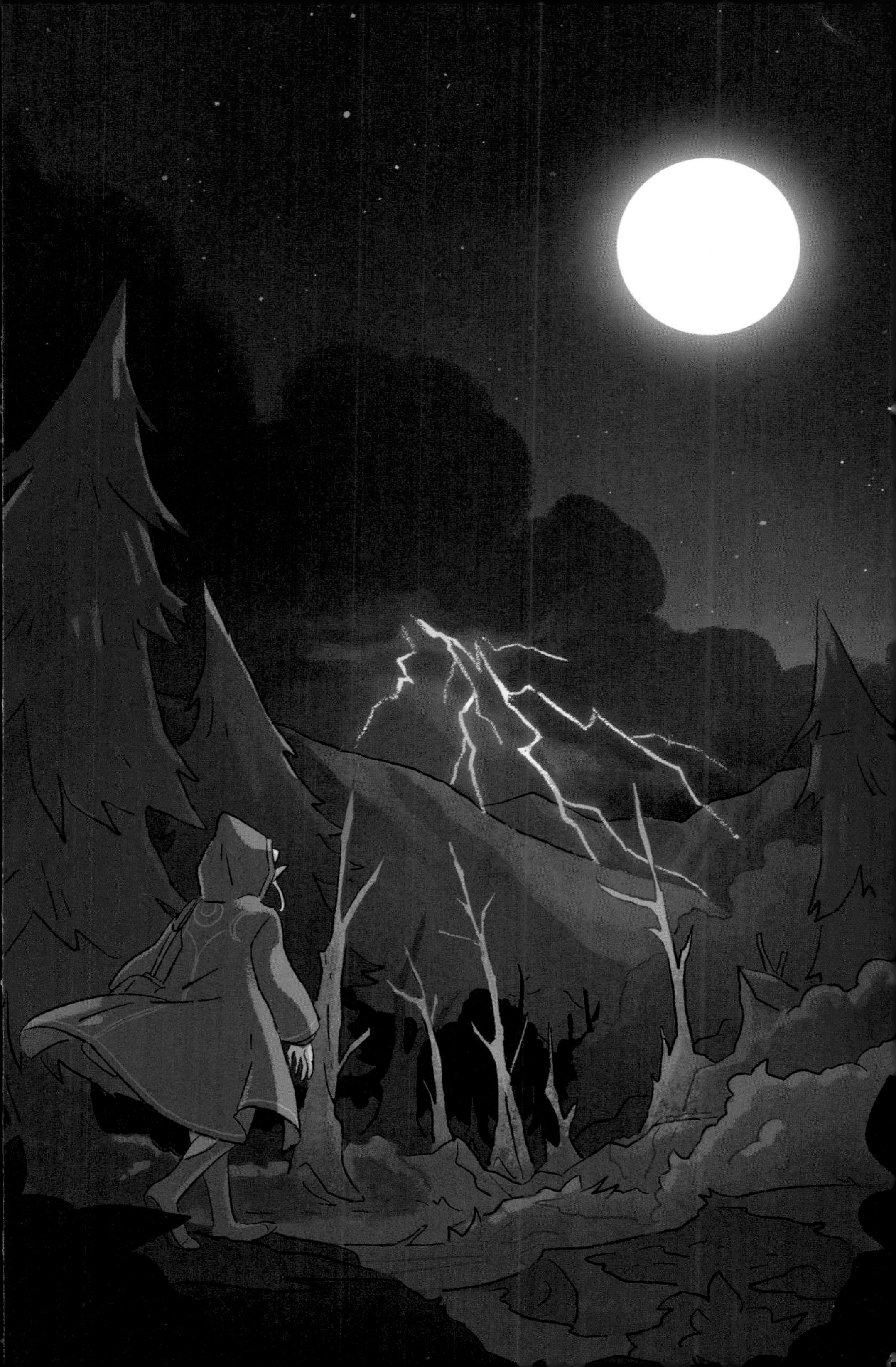

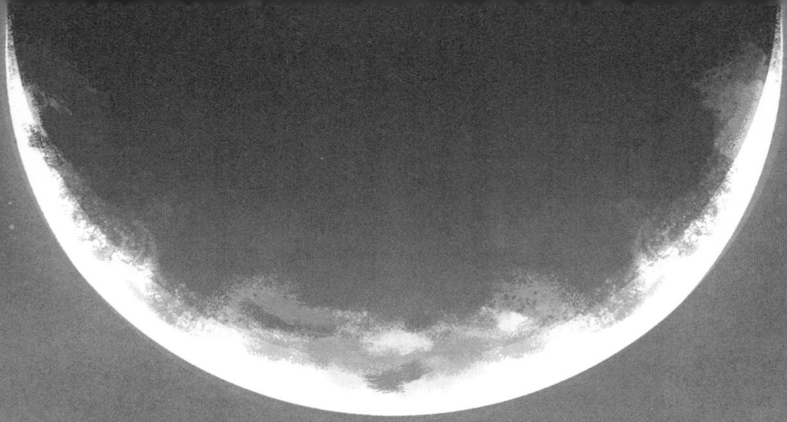

AARON EHASZ and **JUSTIN RICHMOND** are the creators of *The Dragon Prince* and co-founders of Wonderstorm, a media startup in Los Angeles, California. *The Dragon Prince* began as an original animated series on Netflix, and is now being developed into a world-class video game by the same creative team.

Previously, Aaron was the head writer of *Avatar: The Last Airbender*, and Justin was game director on the *Uncharted* franchise.

PETER WARTMAN has been creating stories about monsters, robots, and spaceships since he could hold a pencil. He lives in Minneapolis, Minnesota, where he draws and writes comics pretty much all of the time.

XANTHE BOUMA is an illustrator, colorist, and comic artist for animation and books like the 5 Worlds graphic novel series. Based in Southern California, Xanthe draws inspiration from napping in the beachside sun.